PROJECT CHARON 3: SURVIVAL MODE

PATTY JANSEN

Project Charon 3: Survival mode is also available in audio. Click the image or visit https://pattyjansen.com to find out more.

CHAPTER ONE

TINA PULLED herself hand over hand through the corridor of the Starfighter *Manila*, floating against a very low pull in the downward direction. Now that the ship had stopped accelerating, whatever pull of fake gravity had dissipated and she floated in near-weightlessness. The feeling was odd.

In her own ship, she would have unfolded the rotating habitats and a semblance of gravity would have returned. But the Starfighter *Manila* was very much not her own ship, and giant military ships of the Starfighter class, apparently, didn't hold with such frippery as artificial gravity. Because that was for weak civilians who liked their coffee to stay in their cups and not float through the cabin, like a ticking time bomb, waiting to meet with disaster in the form of someone's head or an instrument panel.

Fancy that.

The people coming up in the corridor behind her, a pitiful bunch of crew Tina had rescued from Aurora Station, were chatting, some of them excitedly because they had never been to the ship's bridge, even though some of them had served on board for a long time. Junior crew just did not come to the bridge, the domain of the captain and flight crew. These women worked in the bowels of the ship and stuck to their stations, adhering to stiff military protocol.

But this was anything but a standard situation.

And excitement wasn't something anyone should feel, at least not if they understood their dire predicament.

Deep shit was an understatement.

Tina wasn't looking forward to telling these women that. They'd escaped from a prison cell at Aurora Station, and any freedom was better than being locked up in the dark with a group of others, right?

Well, maybe.

She floated through the opening into the open bridge space. The emptiness of the room was in stark contrast with how she remembered the bridges and control centres of any large ship or station she had visited to be.

The bridge of the *Manila* was a huge cube-shaped space with control screens along the perimeter. Like every other room in the ship, it had no floor or ceiling, and was designed to be operated from all angles, although there was a ladder in the middle of the room, which seemed to go sideways at an odd angle, but it would go to the direction that was "down" when the ship docked at a station.

Not today.

The workstations hung in a loosely arranged cube formation in the middle of the room, suspended from a framework of metal bars that joined up with the sideways-ladder and criscrossed the space. Each workstation consisted of a Zero-G chair with straps to hold the occupant in their position and one or more work consoles that could be rotated in the desired direction.

Screens of transparent material protected the command panels in the walls from rogue flying objects—or escaped coffee—when the ship made fast moves. The effect was that the bridge's control stations sat inside a transparent aquarium-like cubicle, surrounded by screens that flickered with information.

"Wow," someone said behind her, a young female voice.

Tina knew, having served on these big ships herself, that going to the bridge was a major thing for the low-ranking crew.

Tina let go and floated across to a holdfast post in the middle of the bridge room.

"Wow" did not describe her current reaction. Her feeling was one of sadness and apprehension. This place was supposed to be *busy* and bustling.

But most of the control stations were empty, except for the two most important ones: the first and second pilot stations which faced the opposite wall.

They were occupied by the only two people in this massive room: Aliz, the pilot, and Evelle, Tina's daughter, acting as co-pilot. Aliz had to do two jobs: both fly the ship and give instructions to Evelle, who was normally in charge of navigation but now acted as co-pilot.

There was no one else to do the job. Tina, in turn, had temporarily left her post at the navigation console in order to call the rest of the crew onto the bridge now that it seemed they were safe.

She was exhausted from the strain of having to guide the ship to safety and learning to use the system at the same time. Tina knew about navigation, but nothing about this giant, powerful, deathly and hugely under-crewed war ship felt natural. On top of that, she'd been out of the Federacy Force for over fifteen years and struggled to remember any of the jargon.

They needed resources and people.

That was the predicament they were facing.

The small band of crew all floated into the middle of the room to the holdfast bay, looking around with wide eyes.

They were a sad collection of sixteen people, not even five percent of the crew normally on board this ship.

Aliz swivelled her chair, so she faced the group in the same direction, strapped in to make sure she didn't float away.

Some people acknowledged her with nods. Some others looked simply too stunned to do even that.

Aliz started talking, her voice formal. "Those of you who missed my earlier announcement, welcome to the bridge of the Starfighter *Manila*. It seems we've escaped the station safely, while managing to cool down our overheating engines. Temperatures have returned to normal and we can focus on the next stage. We're down about two thousand crew, so whatever we do from here on is going to be interesting. I'm Captain Aliz Paduano, one of the three first pilots originally consigned to this ship. The other two rotating pilots, Captain Yoshimoto and Captain Menkman, were captured by the pirates and are not with us. Sadly, they were left behind on the station. I have no idea of their fate. This is Flight Officer Evelle Freeman, filling in as co-pilot, because we have no adequately trained people to do this job, so I'll be instructing her. In fact, that should tell you all you need to know about our predicament. Evelle and I will take command of the vessel. Because I am too busy to lead our group as well as look after the ship, the first thing we need to establish is who will lead our operation. I would like to propose Tina Freeman, who is the only reason that we got out of the station at all, and yes you heard that correctly, she is Evelle's mother. I'll hand over to her."

Aliz turned around, attended to something at the controls and swivelled back again while attention of the group went from her to Tina.

"It's an honour to lead you," Tina began. "You don't know me, so here is a small introduction. I'm Evelle's mother. I have a son, Rex, who is still at the station, hopefully soon to be joined by the other two members of the party I was travelling with in my private ship. A long time ago, I used to be a Research Officer with the Force, but I left fifteen years ago, and have been running a security business at Cayelle. How I got to Aurora Station is a long story you may hear one day, when we get the time to sit around and share drinks. I left the Force a long time ago, and I no longer fit the characteristics of a Federacy Officer. I'm not going to run around yelling orders. I'm more interested in keeping as many people as possible in this group alive. Make no mistake, that will be hard enough. So I encourage comments and questions—yes."

A hand shot up.

It belonged to a woman with dark hair in a severe bun and a heavy brow.

"What do you mean when you say *our operation*? Is there an operation?" She seemed very direct.

"Before you comment, state your name and function," Aliz said.

"Yonta Macmillan, dock control officer. I want to know what we're doing, since we have far too few crew members to engage with the pirate fleet."

"The priority is to take us and the ship to safety," Aliz said. "We're not planning to engage with the pirate fleet."

"That seems somewhat optimistic. The fleet might engage with us," said a woman with a loud voice.

"State your name and function," Aliz reminded her.

"Sorry. Sarina DeLeon. Tech Officer second class. Port comms." She had a head full of springy curls and lively eyes that, right now, looked angry.

"The safety of the ship and crew is paramount." Tina repeated Aliz's words.

"So, you're saying we're going to run," Sarina said.

She looked at Tina as if challenging her to argue, but Tina didn't want to give any of the women the faintest skerrick of an idea that getting involved in a fight with the pirate fleet would lead anywhere good. Not with this ship in its current condition.

When the silence lingered, Sarina continued, "Where are we going to run to?"

Tina answered, "I was at Aurora Station because we were underway to Olympus to present information to the Assembly. I would still like to do that. I understand Olympus is this ship's base."

Women looked at each other, uneasy. No one said anything for a while.

That was clearly not the answer they had expected.

"So... we're going to Olympus? Is that the operation?" Sarina asked.

"Why would we do that?" someone else asked. She didn't introduce herself. She was quite young, in her thirties, and wore her sand-coloured hair in a ponytail.

Tina said, "I have some information that I'd like to pass onto them."

"And you can't send it?"

"Don't forget to introduce yourself," Aliz said.

"Sorry. Lisette Mann. Admin officer. I can help if you need something sent. I mean—is it important enough that you need to deliver it in person? Olympus is the official base of *all* Federacy ships. We came out of Pegasus and if we're going back to base, Pegasus would be it, right?" She glanced sideways at Aliz.

Aliz did not react, because she was looking at something on her control panel.

Tina hesitated. *Was* it that important to go to Olympus? Her data was more than fifteen years old. Olympus hadn't wanted her data, even if it had sat in a box owned by the Force for all that time. Was there anyone at Olympus who would care?

She said, "It was why I was here with my private ship. I have a crew member who comes from Olympus and was giving him a ride home. I don't know if it makes sense for this ship to go there. This is why we're holding this meeting. We need to figure out what to do next."

"I don't think we should flee," Lisette continued. Her cheeks were red.

"I agree," said another, louder voice. "Sorry. Zafira Calhoun. Systems Officer First Class. That's IT. I don't know what we're likely to find at Olympus, but I'd very much prefer to stay as far away from that place as possible because it's full of clueless politicians who are as likely to slap some stupid rule on us as I am to accidentally wring any of their necks."

Several other women nodded.

"We can't leave our crew mates," another woman said, who also didn't introduce herself. "I don't like running. I don't like abandoning our mates."

Others agreed.

An uncomfortable feeling came over Tina. Yet she understood the sentiment. "I'm not sure that trying to rescue the others is going to be feasible," she began, picking her words carefully. She didn't know how much these women had seen of what had happened to most of the *Manila*'s crew.

Or if they had seen it, how much they understood. Or even how much they wanted to believe. When Tina had walked through the lab on the way to where the women had been locked up, she had seen all the men and the different stages of their transformation into monstrous beings. She had seen the pirate leader Artan.

But the women had only seen their mates encased in glass cubicles. Imprisoned. They saw their mates needing rescue. Only the ones they could still recognise. Not the ones whose former identities could only be determined from the crew numbers on their uniforms.

When Tina had walked through that lab, she'd had the time to work this out. Once they'd escaped from the prison cell, and the others had been with her, there hadn't been the time for them to wander around, for her to explain or show them.

It was a truth many would find hard to accept.

"I think we should sneak into the station to rescue as many of them as possible," said another woman. "Then we will have more crew to fly the ship." She glanced at Aliz.

"Mention your name and function, please," Aliz reminded her.

"Sorry Clodine Vermont. Weapons tech officer."

She met Tina's eyes in a defiant look. She wore her sand-coloured hair in a tight bun.

"I understand your solidarity with your mates," Tina said.

"Understand? They are our family." Her eyes were fierce. "We should always be there for them. We would expect them to do the same for us."

"We are going to need help before we can take any meaningful action."

"Like what sort of action?" Clodine said. "What does that even mean? Who is going to come to help us? No one else is in this area. Our ship wasn't captured here. The pirates towed us here, because this is their patch of space. I'm not leaving our mates here."

"For one, we can't sneak into the station unnoticed. We can hardly rock up in this ship or the fighter craft in the docking bay."

"Isn't that what the fighters are for? Fighting? We're a fucking war ship."

"Randomly attack a civilian station and cross our fingers that we don't kill the population? There are close to a million people on Aurora Station."

"Who said we were going to do that? We're not dumb. We're trained military officers."

"Yes, in managing the kitchens and admin."

"Who are you to tell us what we can do? You know nothing about us."

"Stop arguing!" Aliz called out.

Everyone fell quiet.

Aliz continued, "You will not interrupt Tina. And also, I will tell you that taking the fighters to the station is futile. They can't take passengers. They're too small and don't have the right docking capability. We have no one to fly them. And the ship is likely to have sustained damage when the engine overheated. We might be able to make evasive manoeuvres if needed, but we're not going to risk a conflict by doing stupid things. No one will be fighting anything."

This was followed by a deep silence.

"Whatever we do, we need to be extremely careful," Tina said, in a milder tone. "We may have one chance at going back for the men, if we think it is feasible and desirable."

"Of course it is desirable," several women said at the same time.

And then Yonta said, "Are we supposed to vote on who is going to lead us?"

"Do you have a problem with Tina?" Aliz asked.

"I'd rather that one of us got the job, because this person would understand what we want. I'd volunteer to take the position."

Some of the women nodded.

One of the men, who had been silent this far, said, "Yeah. I agree."

Tina looked from Aliz and Evelle to Yonta and the other women and the three men.

She let out a breath. "I don't mind. If you think it would be better—"

Aliz interjected. "I'm the highest-ranked officer on board. If you don't like it that Tina leads the group, then I will do it. This is a Federacy Force ship and we'll follow Force rules, which state that in an emergency, the highest-ranked officer will be in charge of decision-making."

"Then why get a non-Force person to lead us?" Yonta said.

"Because Tina knows the area, and she knows more about the pirates than all of us combined. And, as I've already said, I'm occupied with the ship, so I don't want to do it."

"She doesn't understand us."

"Tina is ex-Force. She understands that lower-ranked troops do one thing: follow orders. She tried to be friendly and treat you on an even footing. But since that hasn't worked, you can listen to her, or listen to me, and without me, no one is going anywhere. It's up to you. There is only one thing I will absolutely not stand for, and that is endangering this ship and losing any more crew. Whatever we do, I'm open to suggestions, as long as we adhere to those two things, and as long as we've listened to the advice of people in our group most likely to know what they're talking about."

Her words echoed in the large space. Evelle found something to do on a control panel. The women glared at Aliz, Tina or each other.

For a long time, no one said anything.

No one challenged the leadership. Did that mean Tina was still in charge?

CHAPTER TWO

WELL, that was a rude reminder of how things went in the Force.

Tina had been dumb to start by asking questions. Asking questions was a thing you did when you were on an equal footing. When she was still at Project Charon, she would do it in the lab because everyone there was motivated by science and asking questions was what scientists did. Of course she wouldn't do it with the general station hands. You just told them what they needed to do, and they did it.

Somehow she'd forgotten how officers used to joke at each other to never let the troops lead the way, because you'd end up at the nearest watering hole.

She didn't know why she'd forgotten. Because people outside the military weren't continuously looking for ways to do less, get laid or get drunk?

This was a crash course in reminding her why she left. Or why she never signed up for a position of active duty, but stayed in Research instead.

Well, this was a brilliant start.

She steeled her voice.

"Before we decide what our next step is going to be, we will do a full inventory of all our skills to see how we can make best use of them. I would like you to state your specialty and your name and the function you had on the ship. I'll make notes and compare this against the ship's crew records."

"Why not just get it from the crew records?" Sarina asked.

"Because if you possess any unofficial skills, I want to know about those, too."

"Like knit jumpers or run a marathon?"

"Anything. Please don't be smart."

"I think she means operate machinery we're not licensed to," Zafira whispered loud enough for Tina to hear.

"And then report us to headquarters?" Sarina scoffed.

"If you're doing something that doesn't pass muster, it should be reported," Tina said. "If you spent a bit of time thinking about it, you might figure out why."

Heavens, she'd heard morale had sunk pretty low in the Federacy Force, but hadn't quite thought it was this low. Save their mates so that they could protect each other. Not against an enemy, but against the bureaucracy.

Evelle took out her pad to make notes.

When no one volunteered to start their introduction, Tina pointed to a random person in the group, a young woman with blonde hair and lots of freckles.

"Starting with you. State your name, your function, and any skills you have."

"Are we meant to give rank?" the woman said. Boy, she sounded *really* young and terrified.

"You can, but it's not going to do us any good. We're all in this together, so we might as well forget about ranks for the time being, providing everyone can act like adults."

Yonta glared at her. She had obviously already decided to make Tina's life as hard as possible.

The young woman said, "I'm Gisele Dubois. I'm a kitchen

hand. I do the washing up and stuff. I don't have any special skills. I just signed up because I needed a job."

Next came Zafira. "I already introduced myself. My name is Zafira Calhoun. I work in IT. I run engine diagnostics all day. I'm unbeatable in 3D pool."

A few women chuckled. It was like they still didn't realise how serious their predicament was.

Another dark-haired woman said, "I am Miriam Abadi, Junior Technical Officer. I work in logistics operations, mainly recycling." She was quite short and sturdy, with a thick mop of curly hair that escaped her bun on all sides.

The next woman said, "I'm Rae Yang. I'm a doctor." She was by far the oldest of the ship crew, tough and wiry. Her black hair was peppered with grey. She met Tina's eyes and nodded. She was going to be useful. Tina would ask her to check out the men.

"I'm Clodine Vermont, I work in weapon systems."

"I'm Margot Ford. Cook." Tina was already familiar with Margot, a dark-skinned woman with a smiling face and broad hips.

"Sarina DeLeon, port comms. I know about communication."

"Cally Bennardo. Supply Officer." She was also older. Her voice sounded very sure. "That means I do lots of puzzles of how things fit together."

"Lisette Mann, admin officer, as I said."

That left the three men, who had barely said anything since entering the room.

"What about you?" Tina asked, looking at the first man.

This man held onto the post next to Miriam, and Tina remembered Miriam getting upset about him lying in a pirate's stasis pod. He was sturdy and had dark hair.

"Vito Pellegrini. Health Officer."

"You're a nurse?"

He grinned, showing uneven teeth with a corner broken off one of his front teeth. "Oh, I wish. I could have my hands on these beautiful women all the time."

Everyone seemed to think that was funny.

"I see you've recovered quite well," Tina said, remembering the sarcastic tone that many officers took when someone tried to make fun of them.

"I'm as good as new," Vito said. "It's amazing what a long sleep can do to you."

"Glad that you enjoyed it."

Tina met his eyes squarely. If he was going to joke, she had an endless supply of lame comments she'd perfected on Janusz and other stickybeaks at Dickson's Creek.

But he seemed to shrink.

That reply hit home.

She said, "Our group appears to include a medical officer, so if you experience any lingering issues, I suggest you see her."

He glanced at Rae while remaining silent.

"I'm serious," Tina said, now also looking at the other men in turn.

Out of the three, Vito seemed to have recovered the best.

It gave her hope that they had stopped the transformation process early enough and all of them would recover from having been infected with the alien parasite DNA dust.

"But I repeat, you're a nurse?" Because that would be handy.

Everyone laughed. Miriam put an arm around Vito's waist and patted his chest with her other hand.

Yonta gave her a sharp glance. Most of the ships of the Federacy Force had a non-fraternisation policy. When Tina and Dexter married, they had to ask for special consideration. These two were pushing the boundaries, and some clearly didn't appreciate it.

But Tina had neither the authority nor the inclination to

say anything about it. If it helped Vito recover, let him be with his girlfriend.

"He's a cleaner," Yonta said. She didn't actually roll her eyes, but her voice sounded like she wanted to.

"Yo, I keep your mess tidy."

"I don't make any mess."

A tense silence followed.

Did Yonta get along with anyone?

"What about you two?" Tina asked the remaining two men. Neither of them had said anything. They hung back from the group, as if they didn't want to be here.

She nodded at the first man. He was thin and tall, as was typical for people who had grown up in space. His sparse hair was grey-blond and stood out at odd angles.

"Stan. IT." He sounded as disengaged as Tina remembered IT people to be. They mostly didn't want you to bother them because they seemed to think that general users of computer systems were stupid.

"Do you have a last name, Stan?"

"Sankowki."

"Well, welcome, Stan."

He didn't reply.

Then only one man remained who hadn't said anything yet.

Tina asked, "What is your name? What skills do you possess?"

"Gerry Scott," the man said.

He looked kind of burly and scruffy, with too-long hair and unshaven cheeks. He held himself in place by crossing his arms in front of his chest and around one of the holdfast bars across the cabin.

"What is your field of work?" Tina asked.

"I work in the docks. I do stuff when ships are arriving. You wouldn't understand."

Oh, here we had the "dumb woman" trope.

"I might ask you to try me at some point."

He gave her a wary look.

"Do you have any extra skills that might be useful to us?"

"Not that I can think of."

Great. The group represented one of the most sorry collections of flotsam that she could imagine.

While Tina and the others had spoken, Evelle had been taking notes. She had created a table of names and skills.

Tina looked at her notes, as if something she didn't already know would spring up. The situation was depressing. The group didn't include anywhere near enough people to undertake any activity at all. They didn't even have any of the right people.

"So what is this plan, if I may ask?" Yonta asked.

"I don't know yet. We have to assess the options," Tina said.

Talk it over with Aliz, discuss what they possibly could do.

"The choices are not that difficult, are they? Go back for the rest of the crew or forget about them and carry on?"

"We will assess the options," Tina repeated. "We'll consider the feasibility of each. I'll present the conclusions. Then we'll decide."

But expressions hardened and brows furrowed. Tina hated her own wishy-washy words, but didn't know what else she could say that didn't sound like "we're doomed."

"The decision will be made with the safety of the crew in mind," Aliz said. "As Tina says, we'll first consider all the options."

There was little reaction from the group. Clearly, it was a matter of wait and see for them. If they liked the proposal, they might cooperate. It was time to end the meeting.

"Thank you for coming. I think we all need some rest and a little time for deliberation."

"Yeah, I better do some cooking, I bet you're all hungry," Margot said.

One by one, the group members left the room.

Miriam hung back until the others had gone. She said, "I'm sorry about what Gerry said. I don't understand why he's so cranky. He's normally a very helpful fellow, a friend of Vito's."

Tina hadn't noticed troublesome behaviour from Gerry. She was worried about Yonta.

CHAPTER THREE

AFTER THE WOMEN HAD LEFT, a heavy silence hung over the bridge.

Aliz had turned her attention to the controls.

"Is that Yonta always such a handful?" Tina asked.

"She has a bit of a reputation of being a bitch at the docks," Aliz said.

Evelle said, "But she is very good at her job. Highly competent. She has earned her right to be a bitch. I would never dismiss what she said out of hand."

"I don't dispute that. It's just that she seems to be deliberately stirring the pot."

Tina very much didn't want to mention words like *disobedience* and *disrespect*, but in the time she'd been at Project Charon, behaviour like Yonta's would have earned someone a stern warning.

Evelle said, "I still wouldn't discount what she says."

"What about other people's feelings towards her? Are they likely to agree with her?"

"Quite likely they are, at least the basics."

"You mean—they want to go back to Aurora and rescue

their mates, never mind that many of them are probably dead and others were taken off the station?"

"Something like that."

"But how can they fail to see that we can't make any kind of impression with our small group, and that is if miraculously, we can approach the station without being shot, because everyone will know who we are? If we have any chance of going back, we'll need to wait for reinforcements."

"They might know you still have people at the station you might want to rescue as well."

Rex, Finn, and Thor.

Tina felt sick.

Yes, she did want to return to Rex. She wanted to join up with Finn and Rasa in her ship the *Alethia* and wanted to be on her way. But things didn't always turn out the way you wanted, and she wanted to do silly harebrained things that endangered the people she cared about even less than leaving the system and trusting that they'd meet up somewhere else at some other time.

Aliz continued, "The women are still in shock. Eventually, they will realise that we can't fly the ship with as few people as we have. So they'll want to return to pick up those crew members."

"I thought there was an option to wait for reinforcements?"

"There are unlikely to be any, and they know that."

"Why? Did you hear anything from the fleet? Are they too far away?"

There had been no opportunity to talk about other Federacy ships. Tina presumed Aliz had informed her superior in a far-off fleet about what had happened and had asked for help.

Aliz touched something on the control panel, and several screens before her joined up into one large projection.

"Look at this," she said.

She moved her fingers around, making a point track across the image.

She drew a small circle in the projection. That area enlarged.

"This is a feed I'm getting from our surveillance drone."

The view showed a star field with a few larger specks that were just recognisable as artificial structures. Tina recognised the shape of Aurora Space Station.

Several small specks were hanging around it. She also knew that in this type of projection, the Federacy ships would display the codes next to them.

"Are those all pirate ships?" she asked.

"They could be anything. This feed is not even sending me any probable suggestions. For all I know, they could be merchant ships waiting to be allowed to dock at the station, or they could be hostile. I don't want to make any guesses about their identity."

She shifted the focus to another area, well outside the reach of the waiting fleet.

It showed an asteroid field.

"Some ships of the pirate fleet are hiding in here," she said. "This is where they came from when they attacked us. We can't see how many are in here because the ships are small, and there may even be secret bases inside this field that don't show up in our information either. Who knows?"

She shifted the focus of the projection again, showing one ship in an otherwise deserted field.

"I'm guessing that is us?" Tina asked.

"That's correct. If you peer out the window, you might be able to see this large asteroid that's quite light in colour." Aliz pointed.

"Then where are the Federacy ships? You said you were with the fleet when you were attacked."

Aliz zoomed the projection out again now. A couple of highlighted spots appeared right at the edge of the image.

She pointed. "These are the closest ships. They're the sad remains of our fleet, but they're only a supply ship, a couple of crew ships, a surveillance ship and a fighter carrier ship. They're at least three weeks away. We were captured and towed to Aurora from there."

"But certainly the carrier would still have their fighters?"

"They do, but they're on the way out, because they lost most of their crew in the attack, and they're afraid that if the pirates get hold of the ship, they will steal all the fighters that they don't have the crew to defend. Then we'll be in worse trouble than we are now."

"So, essentially, there is no one to assist us?"

"Pretty much, at least for the time being."

Tina breathed out heavily.

Evelle said, "We must save ourselves, whatever form that's going to take. Because no one is going to do it for us."

Tina said, "So what about we give Yonta the command? If that keeps the peace in the group."

Aliz shook her head. "That would be an exceedingly bad idea. It's you or me. I don't have the time, and I know nothing about the situation at the station."

"But normally the ship's command is not in the hands of the First Flight Officers."

"No, it isn't, but normally the command board makes decisions about the ship. Most of them are not flight officers. One of the flight officers sits on the board. And the board takes our advice seriously. The captain makes the final decision."

Tina drew the obvious conclusion. "And we're missing the captain."

"Yes. She's no longer with us."

A visible shudder went through Aliz, so Tina didn't ask

further. She was still baffled by how the pirates had over-whelmed this huge and powerful ship.

Aliz continued, "The position of the ship's captain is impor-tant both to the leadership and morale of the crew. No, I don't want Yonta in that position. She divides rather than unites. I understand they want to save their mates, but they fail to understand the risks and that they can't just rush into the station, grab the prisoners and rush back out."

"Then how about we get a few others on an executive board to do a better job of explaining this to them?" Tina said. "For example, Rae. She is a doctor, and she is part of the crew. She may be in a position of trust to speak to them."

"You're going to run into trouble no matter what," Aliz said. "Yonta is a powerful and outspoken figure. Most people on board the ship don't express their positions strongly. They're not the personality type. They're in the military. They're not paid to have opinions. They're paid to follow orders."

Tina said, "Just between you and me, if I need to lead this team, I'd like to know what the risks are of taking the ship anywhere. Apart from the obvious—that we don't have enough people to achieve anything—I suspect there is secret tech-nology on this ship, isn't there?"

Aliz hesitated. "There are some things that the pirates would love to get their hands on. That they've been trying to get their hands on already. We have several new and powerful weapons, like our XC7 cannons, and they would also be inter-ested in our engines. Mostly, they would be interested in our habitat regeneration plant."

That was always the issue on board stations and ships. But habitat regeneration on a warship?

Aliz continued, "Mind you, it's not working very well at the moment because we don't have the people to maintain it."

Great. Add another problem to all the ones they already had.

"So your priority is to keep the ship out of the hands of the pirates?" Tina asked.

"That is correct. Not just the pirates. Anyone else."

"I'm someone else."

"Barely."

Tina wasn't sure about that. And there was also the matter of her friends on board the *Alethia* and the fact that she wanted to rejoin them as soon as possible. Although then she would need to say goodbye to Evelle, and she didn't want to do that either.

She continued, "And I guess a secondary priority is to make sure you have enough crew to fly the ship safely."

"That is also correct."

"And you're definitely opposed to going back to the station?"

Aliz let out a deep sigh. "I'm absolutely opposed to any risky missions to save crew we don't even know are still alive. As for going back to the station in some form... we may not be able to avoid it."

"Do you really think that this is all the crew want? To go back to their mates?" Tina asked.

"Yes, they do. You have to understand, their mates are everything to the crew."

"Oh, I understand how everyone in the ship really relies on each other."

"No, things have been quite dire recently, politically. A lot of lost trust and stupid decisions made in the high command, following the orders we've had from the Federacy Assembly headquarters, which have been strange and contradictory. Many people also have lost faith in the Federacy's ability to lead themselves out of this crisis, and the Force has been seen as being too close to the political side of things."

"Any more than usual?"

Tina thought about the building at Olympus next to the

Assembly's headquarters, with its forbidding stone-columned facade. The Federacy Force had a rotating leadership on six-year terms. From Tina's memory, the leadership change happened about two years ago. She stopped following the Force's politics, because the leadership usually kept out of view, the Admiral rarely gave public addresses, and the bureaucratic apparatus that functioned underneath the position of Admiral was considered to be secretive.

Aliz sighed. "There was an instance, not so long ago, where several Federacy Assembly bureaucrats got busted for pushing their own business ahead of a proper tender process. There was an investigation that uncovered a bear pit of corruption. It also involved the Force. Quite a bit more than people expected. Many people were disillusioned and called for corruption inquiries to be held."

"What was the nature of the corruption?"

"It was about a logistics company partially owned by someone in the upper bureaucracy at the Federacy Assembly. They were awarded several civilian and military contracts that were worth a lot of money, and the person stood to make a highly profitable deal. It hit the Force badly in particular. Most of the people on the ground in the Federacy Force are not paid a proper salary. Like us. We receive an allowance and get free food and accommodation for our term of service. Troops got so angry because the Military Services Union has forever been calling to change the rules for space-based crew to be paid properly so that they can purchase investment properties on the stations and can set up ways to survive in retirement. Because this was exactly what the upper command was doing illegally, with funds obtained through corruption."

Yes, Tina well remembered that retirement savings were an issue. The Force's annual retirement fund contribution was such a pittance that it seemed designed to keep people in the

Force for as long as possible. Or at least until their retirement fund amounted to a meaningful sum.

They also had punitive rules about people in the stations being placed with their families. This had always been a point of contention between the troops on the ground and the command. People wanted to be with their families, and the command kept coming up with reasons why this was not possible.

Aliz continued, "This revelation of blatant corruption would have been bad enough in a normal situation, but at the same time, the Federacy came under attack from the pirates at Pegasus Station. The Force only managed to regain control after great loss. The leadership at Olympus was so busy trying to deflect the attention away from their scandals that they didn't react in time to the attack. It was first grade betrayal, and the only people who couldn't see that were the ones directly involved. It was embarrassing, really. So if you think morale was low fifteen years ago, it has become much worse now. The frontline troops declared that they no longer trust the upper command. The commanders from Olympus should have been out there, you know, commanding us, and making plans to defend the Federacy's stations. Instead, they were infighting and covering their butts. Despite the pirate attacks, we're still at that standoff between us and them. In short, this ship's crew is people's family. It's their village. People look out for each other and they want to be looked after by their mates. They're not going to assume that the Federacy will come to help them. They take pride in being self-sufficient and will want to rescue the crew from the hands of the pirates."

"But we need them to understand that the rest of the crew are likely to be dead or have been turned into pirates."

"Yes. In their hearts, some will realise this. But some others will not believe you, no matter how many times you tell them."

CHAPTER FOUR

TINA WAS EXHAUSTED. Now that the immediate pressure was over, she needed something to eat and she needed rest. She asked Evelle where the cabins were and was told to pick one in the officers' section that was located in between the bridge and the mess. There was enough room.

"I'll be sleeping here," Aliz said, jerking her head at the tiny cubicle next to the entrance to the bridge. "Evelle and I are going to take turns at the controls."

"Is there anything I can do?" Tina asked. It felt like responsibility for this enormous ship rested on the shoulders of too few people.

"Later, maybe. Not now."

"Is there anything you need that I can bring for you?"

Aliz replied, "If you could go to my cabin and get the bag that should still be in the cupboard, that would be nice." She tossed Tina a key. "Some food maybe, later."

Tina drifted out of the bridge and made her way through the enormous ship. There were so many cabins that she didn't even hear the other group, which had presumably retreated to the crew quarters as well.

Tina found Aliz's cabin and opened the door.

Wow, people in the higher ranks sure got pleasant cabins, with a single hammock bed, an easy chair, personal communication screens and a foldout desk that could be rotated in whichever direction was the most practical. The cabin had no clear floor. It could be reconfigured according to their travel direction.

Thieves had been in to steal the sheets off the bed, but the cupboard was untouched.

Tina figured that this was because when the ship was docked and took the artificial gravity from the station, the cupboard was on the ceiling. She found the bag inside.

It didn't seem to contain a lot of stuff, but there would be time to go back again if Aliz needed something else.

She left the room and went back in the direction of the bridge.

As she pulled herself through the passage, a door to another cabin slid aside.

The doctor Rae came out.

"Oh, hi," Tina said. She stopped, and a kind of awkward silence followed.

Rae smiled. "I wanted to ask... I was hoping... Would you mind sharing a cabin with me?"

"Me?" Tina was surprised. There were so many empty cabins. Did they even need to share? No one had said anything about where they would sleep. No one had thought much about sleep yet.

"Yes, we're both... of a certain age and I thought we could help each other... you know, when we want to talk."

"Is there anything going on?"

"No."

It sounded too flippant.

"Well... I could."

"Thank you. I'll look forward to it."

"Is it this one?" Tina noted the number on the door: C117.

"Yes. It's not my normal cabin, but it's roomy and there is plenty of space." She hesitated. "Unless you rather stay with your daughter…"

"She's well-looked after at the bridge. It's OK. I'll join you."

"Good. Thank you."

She disappeared back into the cabin.

Now Tina felt unsure about this.

But clearly, Rae had something to say, or something to fear. It could be a personal thing, a youth experience or phobia. It could be something relating to the current crew. Tina didn't like it, to be honest.

She went back to the bridge to deliver Aliz's bag. It would be handy if there was a station other than Aurora close by where the ship could dock, wait for backup to arrive, and she could re-board the *Alethia*.

She wasn't keen to get involved with the Force. The ship had been just a means for her to escape the station. It had been necessary because when the pirates hijacked the ship and docked at Aurora Station, they had neglected to shut off the engines, and they'd been building up power until they were about to explode.

But the *Alethia* was fully stocked and ready to go. Tina could go back to her ship—and leave Evelle to face the problems, like potential engine damage to the ship or the three men turning into mutants, with this fractured group of women?

No, she couldn't do that either.

And should they lock up the men, while they weren't showing symptoms? Not feasible. If the women didn't grasp the situation well enough to understand that going back for the missing crew was likely to be futile, they would never accept that there might be something wrong with the men.

Might be.

No one knew until they showed symptoms. No one knew what the symptoms would be.

Meanwhile, they needed the men because they already had too few crew members on board.

They could wait and see.

But they couldn't afford a situation to develop when they were in mid-space.

So they would have to stay in the vicinity of the station. How long would they have to wait? What was the chance pirates discovered them while they hung around this system?

What *was* the priority for the group?

Going back to the SF *Manila*'s base, at Pegasus Station?

Plain survival?

Finding extra crew?

Warning someone? Who and what was there to be warned about?

Her own mission to go to Olympus and present the Federacy Assembly with outdated data seemed ridiculous. Like they would care about fifteen-year-old data in the current situation.

Then what would she like to do? Go back to Cayelle?

Tina admitted to missing her quiet life, but it would be impossible to go back to her life there while ignoring the crisis.

She should do what Lisette had suggested: simply send the material to Olympus using the ship's secure channels. That would get one thing off her list of worries.

When she arrived at the bridge, Aliz and Evelle still sat at the controls, with Aliz still giving instructions to Evelle. She was going at a crazy pace. Tina stationed herself at another workstation and watched for a while. Aliz was giving instructions on taking control of the ship.

She looked thoroughly exhausted.

"Oh." She had noticed Tina. "Thank you. Just put it in the partition at the back." Even her voice sounded tired.

Tina put the bag in the little cubicle. It was quite cosy, with a single hammock, an entertainment and communication screen and a cupboard for storing personal items. It also contained an environment suit liner and face mask with air canisters.

Tina returned to the central space. She wanted to tell Aliz to have a rest, but she couldn't, because she had to finish the instructions.

Evelle made notes and asked the occasional question. Tina listened, but got lost in the jargon. Her mind wandered off, and she wondered how Rex and Finn were going, and whether Thor and Jens were all right.

"Could you sit here with Evelle?" Aliz asked.

Tina woke up from her daydream. "Oh, yes. Of course."

She let go of the holdfast bar and floated to the co-pilot seat, which Evelle had just vacated when she shifted to the pilot seat. It was still warm.

Evelle had taken Aliz's headset and put it on, her face serious with the concentration of taking on such a grave matter.

"I hope you're all right now," Aliz said.

"Go. Sleep well," Evelle said.

"Please let me know if anything goes wrong."

"We're fine. Go to sleep." Evelle sounded insistent.

Aliz sighed and pushed herself off to the cubicle. She went inside and shut the door.

Tina and Evelle sat in silence.

"How much experience do you have flying this ship?" Tina asked.

"Many thousands of hours. From the safe distance of the navigation station."

"I guess it's different when you sit in the chair."

"Just a little bit."

Evelle glanced aside.

Tina realised how much Evelle was like herself. Pragmatic,

understated. That was probably why they had so many disagreements. She genuinely couldn't remember what any of them had been about. Just that they were always yelling at each other back then.

"Thank you," Evelle said, without meeting Tina's eyes.

"We did nothing special."

"Oh yes, you did. You showed a lot of leadership to the remaining crew. They trust you. I wasn't so sure that they would, but you talk to them straight and get them to follow. They're loyal."

"I'm not so sure about that," Tina said. "I think there are a number of people in that group with big egos."

"There are always those."

"I doubt whether we'll have enough crew to fly the ship for long distances. Aliz didn't tell us what the absolute minimum of crew numbers is."

"That's because it's too depressing."

"I'm guessing we don't have that many."

"It's fifty."

"Shit."

"And they all need to be highly qualified. What is more, we have a very wide range of people. In one way, that would be good. However, we're missing people in maintenance who can do the vital checks on the ship. Aliz wasn't happy with the way the ship handled, and she thinks the overheating that we suffered because the idiots didn't power down the engine has caused some damage to the engines. We don't want to go on any major voyages until it's been looked after."

"Finn is an engineer," Tina said. "He used to work on the large ships."

"That's all very well, but he's not here."

"The *Alethia* is out here somewhere," Tina said. "If we could get him on board, then we would be in a better position."

"That's only one person."

"There is Thor as well. He'd be good to have." Never mind that he was blind.

"It's better than nothing, of course, but normally engineers on board this ship work in teams. The tasks are so big that they are impossible to be carried out by just one person. We would have to go through an extensive training program. We don't have the time and resources to do that."

"So basically we're screwed."

"Basically."

"Is there really anything we can do other than wait for pirates to find us?"

"Trying not to die would be my guess. Contact the Force and hope they'll send ships with replacement crew, although that seems unlikely."

It was well and truly depressing, but what else could they have done? The ship had been overheating, ready to go. If they hadn't taken it out of dock, the engines might well have blown up, with all the associated problems, such as the deaths of a million people at Aurora Station.

It would have solved the question of what to do for everyone, even if not in a good way.

And it would have killed a lot of pirates.

And civilians.

Tina sighed. "I'm going to check on dinner. Do you want anything?"

"Just whatever is on the menu. Margot is an excellent cook. They feed us well on these ships."

CHAPTER FIVE

BUT TINA REALISED with a dark feeling that all the ship's provisions had been stolen while it was in dock at Aurora Station. She had even helped do it.

She pulled herself through the corridors to the ship's galley and adjacent mess, which seemed too large for the few people who were in there.

Margot was pulling open all the storage cabinets, while exclaiming her displeasure at all the things that had gone missing. It was hot in the kitchen, and Margot's face shone with sweat.

"They instructed the crew from all the merchant ships on the station to come here and raid the food storage for their ship supplies," Tina said.

"Who? The station managers at Aurora?"

"Yes. There was a long wait to get ship supplies and many merchants and private vessels wanted to leave, but the Ship Supply Office kept us waiting because they had no supplies. When this ship was brought in, we all got orders to get our supplies out of the ship. They had lines of people going in here.

Entire families turned up. We went inside as well. People were getting whatever they could lay their hands on."

"Well, fuck that," Margot said. "That means we can't go far. We have some stuff, but meals are going to be interesting. And we'll run out of food soon."

"We still have these," Gisele said, holding up the flat packets. Tina remembered seeing them, but no one in the group of people who had been raiding the kitchens had known what to do with them. They looked like flat pancakes wrapped in foil.

It was quick-bake bread.

After a short while in the oven—which looked too huge for the paltry amount of food—the packets expanded into loaves of freshly baked bread.

Margot made a soup of various kinds of frozen vegetables.

The Zero-G environment required it to be served in cups with drinking spouts.

It was thick and hearty and made her feel warm.

Lisette was also there, and Tina asked her how best to word her message to Olympus. Lisette said to come and see her later so she could help.

When Tina finished, she brought portions to Evelle and Aliz. Evelle sat alone at the controls. She took the container with a smile. Aliz was asleep, so Tina put the food in the container next to the door so she could warm it up later.

Tina was tired, but she felt she needed to speak with Evelle, because the long years of no contact hung like a heavy weight between them.

But it was hard to know what to say, or even where to start.

A lame "I'm sorry" didn't cut it with someone who should have been yours to look after, but who had slipped from your grasp before you'd been able to to help her. Someone who, in Evelle's rebellious past, didn't want to be looked after, but had probably been crying out for help of a different kind as the one provided by Tina and Dexter, if only Tina had been smart enough to see it.

What was there to apologise for if you still didn't see how you could have done anything differently?

So they sat in silence for a long time.

After a while, Evelle said, "Why did you go to Cayelle?"

Tina shrugged. "It was out of the way. I left everything relating to my Federacy position in the locker at Kelso Station..." Where it had sat untouched for fifteen years. "I wanted a place that had some natural life. I didn't want to return to Tirkala." And incur the scorn of her family, her brothers, her cousins, who all lived and died by the size of their incomes and their houses.

"And you lived there with my brother, or half-brother?"

"No, he's your full brother."

Tina had never been interested in forming another close relationship with a man.

"Has Dad ever seen him?"

"Not that I know. I'm pretty sure he hasn't."

"He's... disabled, right?"

"Don't say that to his face, or he'll break your bones with his metal hands. Here, that's him in his new harness."

She showed Evelle the picture she had taken in the shop at Kelso Station when Rex first got his harness.

Evelle nodded. "I've seen people wear those things. They're impressive. They're usually battle veterans."

Not kids born without limbs because of the stupidity of their mothers.

"I didn't know I was pregnant, so I did some things I wouldn't have, had I known."

"That must have been terrible, I mean—when he was born."

"It was, in a way. I'd not looked after myself. To be honest, I didn't want him. My marriage had broken down, and I didn't want to be saddled with a baby. For the first few weeks after he was born, all I wanted to do was kill him."

She shuddered inside when thinking back to that time, and wasn't proud of her initial feelings towards Rex. She didn't want a baby. If she'd chosen to have a baby, she didn't want a boy, and she definitely didn't want a boy with disabilities.

"But you didn't," Evelle said, still looking at the picture.

A small light started blinking on the ship's controls and she pressed a few buttons with confidence, as if she piloted a high-tech battle ship every day.

"Of course I didn't kill him. I knew I could never do that. But then I still faced having to look after him. Cayelle is not a rich world and technology is backwards. Everything costs a fortune. I wanted to give him a decent life. So I worked for him. I started the shop and changed the old house so that he could move around. He can run most of the shop by himself. I was very keen to make sure he could survive independently. I'm about two-thirds of the way there."

"Wow. Dad always said you had the baby just to extract payments out of him."

That was something Dexter would say. "Dexter only ever paid for his very first harness. Nothing else."

"Are you still in contact with him?"

"No. What about you?"

"I received some correspondence from him a few years back. It was about what I wanted done with my things in the apartment after the project and the station had closed."

"What did you say?"

"I told him I didn't care. Whatever still was in my room that I left as a fifteen-year-old, I hadn't missed. But he packed up a box of things and sent it to me, anyway."

Tina was surprised about that. She hadn't thought Dexter would do that sort of thing. "Really?"

"I think he was sad that the project closed, and he sounded

kind of sad that he hadn't seen me for so long. I mean—he didn't say so in so many words, but just the tone of his message made me think that. He *wanted* to send me the box, so he sent it, even when I said it wasn't necessary."

"What was in it? "

"Some photographs of... you know, us, when I was young." When they were still a happy family. "Also... do you know those pillows I used to have? The ones with the cats on them?"

Tina remembered. Evelle was always so keen to have a cat, which of course was not allowed on a military station. When she was very young, she had a lot of trouble accepting this. Evelle always said that she hated where she lived and she wanted to live in the places where her friends lived, big space stations with normal schools, where people had cats. Of course, then she had to sign up with the army.

"Do you still have those pillows and the photographs?"

"I do, but they're in storage," Evelle said.

"Where?" Like, where had she spent the past fifteen years? Was there a partner somewhere in another place?

"At Pegasus Station."

This was a major military training base. So maybe not. Maybe the constant tension between her and Dexter had damaged Evelle's ability to form relationships.

"Did you live at Pegasus?"

"Yes, for about five years. I used to run training courses in navigation until the pirate situation escalated and we were all put in active duty."

Her voice held a tone of sadness, but Tina didn't know how to ask further without feeling like she was prying.

Tina asked, "Have you ever been back to Project Charon?"

"Yes, I went back for a visit after you left. I wasn't sure what I'd find, but it was just before the project closed. Even though at the time we didn't know that was about to happen."

"Why did you go?"

She shrugged. "I was in the area. That's what people do, right? Visit the places where they'd grown up when they're in the area?"

The fragile look on her face cut Tina inside. But she didn't want to give in to the gulf of deep emotions that opened up in her.

"How long ago was that?"

"About ten years ago. The project was a very different place. It felt very industrial, as if they were running a commercial lab or something. You know Dad's office up in the area we used to call the bird's nest?"

Tina nodded.

"It was all gone. They'd turned it into some sort of equipment room. I wasn't allowed to go in. Your office was still there, but there were three people in it. I didn't recognise any of them, so I didn't talk to them. I did go into your division and your lab, and most of it was empty. There were not many people around, anyway. Most of the people who were there didn't really want to talk about you, and the ones who did were very hostile."

There was a disturbing tone in her voice that indicated that had Tina still been around when Evelle came, they might have made up. She had been looking for her mother.

Tina went up to Evelle and put an arm around her shoulders, which was awkward in Zero-G. Her shoulders were hard and bony under her uniform.

Evelle reached out and touched Tina's hand.

"We are here now, we'll soon be reunited when Rex comes to the ship." She hoped that was going to happen.

"Except for Dad."

Yes, that was always a painful subject.

Tina said, "Do you have any idea what happened to him? Did you see him when you visited?"

"No, he had left, but I knew that already. It wasn't a pleasant visit because no one wanted me, no one still remembered me. I didn't stay long."

"Did they at least tell you what happened to Dad?"

Evelle stared at Tina. "I thought you knew."

"I don't. He just stopped replying to updates I sent him about Rex."

"Surely he's still alive?" She looked haunted.

"I don't know. I don't know how to tell you this nicely, but I have my suspicions that your dad was involved, either on purpose or accidentally, in starting up the pirate army."

"What?"

"The material that causes people to become grotesque monsters came out of a rift to another universe or another dimension or whatever it is, we don't know. At Project Charon, we captured some dust and were doing experiments with it. I worked with this material. It was showing promise as being a genetically healing material, and we were working with it. But we had a lot of problems with sickness at the station. That's how we discovered that it changed people into the creatures we now call pirates."

Evelle's eyes widened. "You mean those horrid creatures with the grey warty skin were once normal people who have been changed deliberately?"

"I don't know that it's deliberate for *them*. But definitely it had something to do with the process being set in motion by other people. We have already seen that with all those cubicles in the pirate section of Aurora Station. And as far as I know, your dad was the first person involved in selling this material. He may have been set up or forced to do it, and he might not have been aware of what he was selling, but he definitely did it."

Evelle's eyes were wide. "But wasn't Project Charon a secret military station?"

"Yes, but even the military might have sold it to interested parties. It is fairly common to subcontract parts of projects like this. The material showed promise as a catalyst to regrow faulty and missing body parts. The military would have contracted that out, because they don't have the expertise to do this type of work themselves, but it was done too quickly, without proper investigation into any other effects, such as how to stop extra mutations taking place."

"Did you always know this?"

"It was an important reason your dad and I broke up. I didn't agree with him going to this conference to talk about our work, and I didn't feel we were anywhere near ready to fulfil any of the promises that he and others were making to interested parties about this magical material."

"He might just have needed the money. I heard that when I was at a Project Charon, money was a big problem. They failed to receive funds they needed for the project, and they were looking for alternative ways of funding it."

"Most likely, someone in headquarters realised how dangerous this material was and was trying to shut down the trade."

"And in doing so they actually encouraged it."

Tina took a deep breath and nodded. "This is why I'm interested in what happened to Dad."

Evelle met her eyes, and a look of horror came in them. Tina didn't need to mention her fear, that Dexter had become a pirate himself, irrevocably changed by the material from the rift into a killing heartless monster.

"I want to know where he is, so I don't need to be afraid that he will end up on my doorstep."

"Last I heard rumours of Dad was about six or seven years ago," Evelle said. "Do you think he remarried?"

"I doubt it. He was never that sort of person."

"If you knew where he was, would you see him again?"

"Only to know that he was OK. I wouldn't be interested in meeting him."

"I really don't know. I'm sorry."

They were silent for a while.

Then Evelle said, "What about my brother? Where is he?"

"I left him at the station with a friend of his and the friend's father."

"I thought you had a ship, and he was on it."

"Not that I know. The ship left with the other two members in our party: the engineer and a stray girl we picked up at Kelso Station."

"Do you know where the ship is?"

"They're likely to be around here, waiting for us or looking for us." Or so she hoped.

"Can you contact them?"

"Wouldn't that give away our position? I'd hoped they would contact us first."

"That would also give away our position. We're going to give away our position no matter what. We can't keep silent. We'll have to start doing something. I think it's a good idea to contact them."

"I'd still like to clear it with Aliz," Tina said.

"Yes, that's probably a good idea."

CHAPTER SIX

TINA MADE her way back to the kitchen because she wanted to get something to drink before going to bed. It was very quiet in the ship, but Margot was still cleaning up and rearranging her supplies, still muttering about how few items they had left and how poor the choice was. Another person who was still at the holdfast bar in the middle of the room was Lisette.

"Did you still want me to help you send that message?" she said.

"That would be nice," Tina said. "Even if you could just show me how to do it. I'm not sure that I have everything ready. Some material might still be on my ship. I may have to think about exactly what to say, but it would be nice to learn how to do this."

They both took their tea and Tina followed Lisette through the corridors of the ship.

They passed through several sections that had clearly contained administrative offices. The rooms were now dark and computer screens idled, and no one worked at the workstations.

Tina wondered why a ship like this would need so much

administration, but then again, they normally had over two thousand people on board, and those people were sure to need to send messages and file reports.

Lisette took her into one of those offices.

She crossed to a workstation and brought it to life with a touch of her fingers. Tina hung onto the back of the chair, looking over Lisette's shoulder.

"We have access to the Force's most secure communication system," Lisette said. "Anything we say in here gets reported straight to the Admiral."

"Is this how Aliz has contacted the rest of the Force?"

"It is."

"And she hasn't received a reply yet?"

Tina didn't like the chance that she would reach someone who cared about her data with this system. This was an emergency channel. They would just laugh at her fifteen-year-old data. She told Lisette.

"There is someone at the other end who files all the incoming messages into different sections," Lisette said.

"And they have the power make someone reply?" Tina said.

"They *will* reply."

"Before I left the Force, I told them where I'd left my full report and told them it contained important data. It was not data they would like to hear, but they should have collected the report. They didn't. Fifteen years later, it was still there. I don't want the same to happen when I send it now. It *is* important. There may be information in it that will allow the Federacy to stop the spread of mutations."

"People will see the message. I can guarantee that. The people at the other end of this system take their jobs very seriously. They're coveted positions. I know because I used to work there. Everyone is always trying to get the Admiral's ear, and sometimes people are willing to bribe quite a big sum of money to get it. You have to be strong-minded to resist it, and even then you can sometimes get into trouble. We took pride in having high integrity and making sure that every message gets seen. Things may have changed since I left, but that would have stayed the same."

Lisette told her how to use the system, and gave her a password, and told Tina that she could come in here at times that everyone else was awake, and she could send her material securely.

"I will write up my message and will send it in one of the few coming days," she said. "It's not as if we are going to be very busy."

Lisette smiled, and the moment between them was distinctly uncomfortable.

Tina returned to her cabin. She dreaded what she was going to find there.

Rae had said little during dinner, and Tina had no idea why she had asked her to share a cabin. She hoped Rae would not be one of those really insecure people who needed to be talked into doing anything, because she didn't have the energy.

And also she hated herself for thinking that, because, put like that, it sounded really callous.

It was just that Tina was coming to the end of her own reserves, and she didn't want to deal with yet another person's troubles.

When she came into the cabin, Rae was hanging up in her sleeping bag watching some sort of entertainment vid.

The room contained two beds, each underneath a storage shelf with neatly folded uniforms, tanks, EVA suit liners, helmets, flexible environment suits and a small cupboard for personal items, all strapped down against weightlessness with netting.

A small desk sat against the back wall, crowded in between the beds. A wallscreen occupied the wall space above it and flickered into life when Tina came in, reminding her of the canteen menu.

"Stupid thing," Rae said. "I'll find out how to turn it off."

"Wow," Tina said, floating into the middle of the room. The beds were like hammocks: you had to fold the net around yourself so you didn't go floating around while asleep. "I'd forgotten how small these cabins are."

And even the screen was something she remembered. You could set it to a variety of pretty landscapes on a variety of settled worlds. Its primary function was to let the room's occupants experience a sense of direction.

"This is a cabin for officers First Class. They have a lot more room than us mere mortals," Rae said. "My regular cabin has only a bunk bed and two tiny personal lockers at the end. The screen is in the wall next to a recess for the suits."

Tina floated across the cabin. "Which cupboard is mine?"

"Take your pick. They're both empty."

"You haven't brought your things here?"

"I've been busy checking up on everyone in the clinic."

"We can get your stuff," Tina said.

"That's not really necessary," Rae said. "I'll get it tomorrow. I don't own much stuff."

"You said your cabin is smaller?" It was hard to imagine. "These ships really don't leave much room for personal items."

"No, they don't. You get used to it."

Tina tried to find somewhere to leave her shoes so they wouldn't float away.

"Are you all right?" Rae asked.

Tina wasn't sure how to take that question.

"Where do you leave your shoes?"

"You'll find hooks on the inside of the cupboard door."

Tina opened the door. Rae was right.

She hung up her shoes.

"Wow, I'm tired," she said.

She hoped that would signal she didn't want to talk about personal problems.

But Rae continued, "It's so nice to you have your daughter here."

"Yes."

Definitely not going there.

"Are you happy about the group?" Rae asked.

"Whether or not I'm happy about it, there isn't anything I can change about it, isn't there? We are stuck with the people we have."

"Do you think any of them are less committed to getting us to safety?"

Tina turned around and met Rae's eyes.

"I've only known these people for a couple of hours. I can't really make that kind of judgement. Sure, some people seem to bicker about everything, but that might be because they're stressed, or because they are normally like that."

She was highly tempted to ask where she was going with this questioning, but she also really wanted to go to sleep.

She took off her over clothes and unzipped the sleeping bag.

Her muscles still remembered how to get into one of these and how to do up the fastening without floating away again. It was amazing. It was like at least seventeen or eighteen years ago that she had last done this during her extended travel on one of the long distance trips. This was also why, when she left Project Charon, she had bought a ship with revolving habitats. Living in zero gravity was annoying. Really annoying.

Tina hesitated. "Do you want me to turn off the light?"

"Sure. I'll be watching this for a bit, but I can watch it with the light off."

Tina snuggled up in the sleeping bag. But she found it hard to get comfortable.

The headrest was too much inflated, and she searched around for the button to reduce the air pressure in the cushion.

"It's on the other side," Rae said.

So she was not really watching what was on the screen and that was casting flickering coloured lights over her face.

There was silence again for a while, but Tina found it hard to get comfortable. What really bothered her was the expectation that Rae would start asking questions.

She might as well get that part out of the way.

"Look, you might just want to tell me what's on your mind, because I won't be able to sleep if I'm expecting you to come out with it, anyway. Why did you ask me in particular to stay in your cabin? I'm exhausted, so just give me the short version, whatever it is."

She had half expected Rae to get angry, or be insulted, but she laughed instead.

"You're just as direct and smart as they all said you were."

"They?"

"People who know you. People who wondered what happened to you after you left Project Charon."

That got Tina's attention. "Who are you in contact with?"

"Several people who were at the project. Levi Mann, Wilfred Schmitt, Gloria Alvarez."

Tina's heart melted at hearing those names. They were people about whom she had sometimes wondered what had happened to them, people who used to work in the lab with her, and she had left behind, without telling any of them where she had gone. They were dear colleagues, who she used to laugh with and play games with after hours.

"You're working with all of them?"

"Well, not working. But I am in contact with all of them, and they wondered how you are. That's why I asked you to share. Because it's not general knowledge that I'm in contact with those people."

"What are they all doing?" To be honest, after speaking to Arkady on Aurora Station, she'd had the feeling that most of the people who worked at Project Charon were dead, but clearly that wasn't true. Maybe it applied only to the scientists.

"Most of them have gone to civilian jobs. Many of them still work in science, but Gloria has become a schoolteacher."

Tina nodded. She was always going to do that. Gloria was great with children.

"But what are you doing as a ship's doctor while you're in contact with all these interesting people?"

"I don't work with them. They are just in an organised group I'm a member of. We're like... skeptics, not taking the Federacy's word as gospel. We talk a lot, but it doesn't pay. I still need a job."

"Do you know Arkady Dimitrov?"

"I know him very well. Yes, he is also in the group."

Tina could hit herself over the head for not spending more time with Arkady and that group, but also knew there hadn't been the time, and other concerns had been more important.

Rae continued, "My family lives at Olympus and I had no intention to stay in that cesspool of corruption and go down the same path as my father."

"He was not one of those politicians who was caught bribing?"

"Oh goodness no, he wasn't a politician, but he was working in that troublesome area, and the temptation to accept money to allow people to do things that shouldn't be allowed was great. You would never have heard of my father. The whole Medical Approvals Board is basically one large, secretive organisation. But they wield the kind of power that stops or makes laws."

Tina felt cold. "You're not saying your father had something to do with the spreading of this supposed medicine that was going to cure a bunch of diseases, but that ended up turning people into pirates instead?"

"Not directly, not that I'm aware of. But indirectly, they were all responsible. They're power hungry. They want to line their pockets with money from the large pharmaceutical companies at Olympus. They are aware it's dangerous. They know the mutation will slowly creep through the society, turn people into monsters and they don't care, because it will happen after their time, because they're old men. And some of them even think the mutations benefit humanity. I asked you to share my room, because I want to warn you. Betrayal is everywhere. Your husband Dexter was but one of the first few. As it caught on that there was big money to be made with spreading this stuff because of the promise to grow spare body parts, many people jumped on. There will be sympathisers in the crew of this ship. Why else do you think this ship fell into the hands of the pirates?"

"I had wondered about that. You don't think anyone deliberately passed the ship into pirate hands?"

Aliz certainly knew nothing about that, or she would have told Tina.

Rae shook her head. "I've never discovered that anyone did, but it wouldn't surprise me."

"Who would do something like that? Haven't they heard the stories of what happens at stations like Aurora?"

"Money, power and greed. Many of those on board with dubious connections are still in pirate captivity, but I would never trust everyone currently on board the ship."

And the women wanted to go back to rescue these people, while some of them might already have sided with the pirates.

THE RADIO CRACKLED in Tina's headphones. She watched the screen while the search beacon scanned the space around the ship in ever-increasing circles.

"Come on, come on."

Her hands were sweaty on the controls. The last she'd seen of her ship was when Finn and Rasa left. She didn't know whether the *Alethia* was still hanging around the station, or whether they had moved to a different area.

"Come on, come on."

How long would this take?

The beacon focused on a spot on the screen. Tina's heart jumped. She recognised the ID. The scanner had found the ship.

Her headphones crackled again.

"Finn, can you hear me?" Aliz had told Tina not to use the ship's identification.

A male voice replied, "I'm not Finn."

Tina flooded with relief. Rex was at the controls. That meant they'd met up.

He continued, "I can get Finn on, but I would think you were happy to talk to me."

"I am happy to talk to you," Tina said. "I was afraid that you were still at the station with Jens and Thor."

"Yes. But Finn came back to pick us up. We are still going to Olympus, right?"

"Well, I have no idea. First, I need to get off this ship to you. We're not in great shape and I don't know if I can leave the crew a navigator short while they're already heavily under-crewed. I don't want to separate the family again. Your sister won't want to come with me, because she has a job at the ship, and that's going to be hard enough. We'll have to make a decision one way or another, but we'll need to talk about it with everyone involved. What about you, how were things at the station?"

"It got a bit crazy. For the first night after you left, I was sitting in Jens' room fiddling with the computers, but someone must have figured out that it was us messing up their security systems, so they came to the door and questioned us. We pretended we didn't know anything, but Jens' dad decided that we had to go. So we went to this other guy's place for a bit. It was Arkady or whatever his name is. Do you know what a cool computer lab he has? You should see all the things he can do. It's amazing."

"Is he on board the *Alethia* with you?"

"No, he decided to stay at the station. There are a number of other people, you know, those who came to that meeting at Jens' place."

Damn it. The *Manila* really could have used some people with more advanced skills than doing admin or being a kitchen hand.

"What is the situation on the station?"

"When we heard that Finn was coming back in, we tried to get out to the docks, but there were guards everywhere, so Jens' dad made up some kind of emergency he had to fix for Finn and we had to dress up in overalls to be his assistants. And then we managed to get into the ship."

It seemed that even though he was blind, Thor had ways to get into everything. Maybe because he was blind. People didn't think he was harmful.

"And what have you been doing since?"

"Waiting for you to show up. Finn says a ship like the *Manila* is very well shielded and doesn't normally put out a call sign. He's been teaching me to sit here while he's asleep. Thor has been cleaning up everything. You should see how clean the storage compartment looks now."

Tina laughed. "The storage compartment? We're not even using that."

"That's what I told him, but he wanted to do it, anyway. He says he can't stand mess."

"It was not that messy."

But Tina remembered how Finn and Rex had held a pissing contest in the storage hold, and there were probably quite a few things in there that she never used. It might be a good idea to have an inventory to know what was at their disposal and what they might still need to get.

That also required thinking about the future, and that was something she was going to have to do.

"So it's just you and Finn and Jens and Thor."

"And Rasa."

Damn, yeah, Tina had almost forgotten about Rasa and her pets.

"Is Rasa all right?"

"Yeah, she's fine. The geese as well, but they're getting very cheeky. We have to make sure they don't get out of their cage because they can't fly in weightlessness. They keep bumping into everything. They shit everywhere."

"Sounds like fun."

"At least they keep the cactuses at bay. The things are growing like crazy."

"Are they? Who is looking after them? Did the geese finally decide they didn't want to eat them anymore?" Tina laughed.

"It's actually not really funny, but quite strange."

"What do you mean?"

"The geese are eating the cactuses. I don't know if it's because of that, but they developed all these strange feathers. They don't look like geese any more."

"What do you mean? How can they not look like geese?"

"I don't know. They started changing bit by bit. The feathers started going curly, and then random patches of colour started appearing on their back and wings. Their beaks went funny. They don't look like geese any more. More like some kind of weird parrots."

"Do they still lay eggs?"

Before he could answer, Tina had already decided to tell him that if they did, not to eat them. In fact, she was quite keen to tell them to get rid of these animals, even though that decision would probably not be popular with Rasa.

"Yes, they've gone crazy. We've got more eggs than we know what to do with. They're all different colours, too. White ones and blue ones and pink ones and speckled ones."

"Don't eat them."

"Why not? They're good. They make the constant supply of curry bearable."

"Have you been eating them all the time?"

"Yes, just like when you were here with us."

"And you haven't noticed anything funny, like skin rashes or anything like that?"

"No. Although Rasa says she's sick of eggs, but Finn, Thor and Jens love them. It's incredible how bad the supply situation was at Aurora—has been for months. They barely get any decent food. Just the protein cubes, and even those are hard to get."

"And Jens and Thor haven't been getting unusual symptoms either?"

"From eating eggs?"

"Just in general."

"No, we're fine."

Tina was glad for that. "I still think you should stay away from the geese, and not touch them with your bare hands, definitely don't let them nibble at you."

"Oh no, their beaks are really keen, and we stay well away from them. They have taken over the room with the cactuses."

"What about the cactuses?"

"They've gone berserk, too. The geese can't stop eating them, and they're growing all over the place. I don't know how they grow, because we don't water them that much. They seem to grow by themselves, and they move all around the place. They don't seem to mind being eaten. They've grown into hedges. We can't get into the storage cabinets against the side wall anymore. At least not until someone finds the machete."

"I'm pretty sure the machete is still in the tool shed at the shop in Dickson's Creek."

"I was wondering about that."

"Just make sure you don't let the cactuses escape that room. Not the geese either."

Tina was highly tempted to tell him to clean the room out and incinerate the lot, but that would probably not go down well with Rasa. This news worried her. She wanted to be back on the ship.

Rex said Finn had woken up and wanted to speak to her. There was some rustling as he took the earpiece off and gave it to Finn.

"Tina, I'm glad to hear that you made it. How is everything?"

"We managed to get out, but it looks like we might have some damage to the engines. We desperately need engineers. We are desperately under resourced and understaffed. The captain isn't sure whether we can make any long distance voyages."

"Does the ship have any docking facilities for mid space?"

"I think we do, but I don't know how well it is suited to non-military vessels."

"The fighters normally don't have soft docks. You don't want to have to break free from a cloud of hangers-on when you have to move suddenly."

That made sense to her. "How is the *Alethia*?"

"Doing well. I think Thor has managed to fix our power issues. We haven't had any more problems."

"When did you leave Aurora?"

"We went back for a quick visit to pick up Rex, Jens and Thor. I didn't think you'd mind. We heard that Aurora Station had reopened, and merchants were allowed to come in. We qualified as a commercial ship and were allowed to dock. I'm sure Thor had something to do with the dockside part of the process."

Yes, Thor had been very useful.

"What is it like on the station?"

"It's pretty quiet. They've been keeping all the residents in their apartments. Most of the businesses are closed, except for the essential shops. But most of them are delivering things to people's apartments so they don't have to go out."

"Have you seen any indication of how many people Artan has brought in or out?"

"I think they're trying to manage the public part of the station with a minimum number of people. We've seen a number of ships leaving the station, but it's hard to see what is in them on the flight system, unless they state their purpose, which they usually don't. But I've been trying to keep an eye on them from here."

"What about any others?" Like military ships.

"A number of Freeranger merchants are still around. Probably hanging around to wait until they come back to continue whatever commerce they're involved in. They don't seem to be afraid of the pirates. But it's quiet. It's like everyone on the station is waiting for something to happen."

"Have you been able to scan any activity in the other half of the station after we left?"

"Nothing that is particularly informative."

"Has the station director given any more speeches?"

"Just a very short one, to tell everyone to comply with the authorities' demands and stay inside and that people would be safe if they did that."

She could hear the scorn in his voice. The station's director, Zia Partlow, was Finn's ex, and appeared to be solidly under pirate influence.

Tina could only imagine the level of worry in the station once it came out that there was a substantial part of the station occupied by a pirate army, but then again, people at Aurora Station had been living like that for a while already.

It occurred to her that although Artan might have captured the *Manila*, he didn't seem particularly interested in starting an all-out battle. It was hard to figure out just what he wanted, other than turning military personnel into grey-skinned, tentacled monsters that enjoyed fighting and didn't mind dying for their commander.

Tina and Finn agreed that they should investigate how to join up and that they would speak later.

Then she signed off.

Behind Tina, Aliz said, "He's right. We don't have a soft dock, but we can take smaller ships into the internal dock."

"The *Alethia* isn't a small ship," Tina said.

"Isn't it a merchant vessel?"

"Yes, but it has two revolving arms and four habitats."

Aliz whistled between her teeth. "Give me the specs and we'll see what we can do."

Tina chatted a bit more about Rex and Finn. Aliz took a lot of interest in Finn's previous position as ship engineer.

"We could use one of those, to be sure," she said. "I'm trained to do some emergency maintenance myself, but there are parts of the ship I wouldn't touch. Your engineer is likely to be accredited for only a very small section of engine maintenance, but he'll have had training in all of its operations, which is more than I can say about myself."

"How many engineers would you normally have on board?"

"Ten or twelve."

"Shit. But two is better than none, right?"

"Two?"

"The other guy, Thor, is a civilian engineer. At some point he used to be in the military, but his eyesight was damaged."

"He's blind?"

"As a bat, but he's amazing. You'll understand when you see him work."

"Hmmm." Aliz clearly wasn't convinced.

"So we'll try to join up?" Tina asked, feeling hopeful. She missed them. Rex could be stubborn and Finn had his moments, but she wanted to be back on board the ship and on their way to Olympus. Her talk with Rae last night had only made her more determined that if she was going to get her information to the Federacy Assembly, sending it through the Federacy's system was *not* going to be the way to do it.

"Try, yes."

Aliz had pulled out a schema of the ship, with the docks marked, and then enlarged that area.

Tina looked over her shoulder. She hadn't been to that part

of the ship, but remembered seeing the dark hall with the fighters in passing.

Aliz explained. "Normally we can take in several small ships. We have some fighters still on board, and I don't want to jettison any of them. We might still need them."

"Do we have pilots capable of flying the fighters?" Tina asked.

"None that the ship can spare, but they're valuable assets and the command would hate it if they fell into the hands of the enemy."

"Do you need the space in the hall where those ships are?"

"I hope we won't, but we may have to reconfigure the surrounding docks. We can move this wall and this wall outward." She pointed. "We need to figure out how many people we need to do that, and if anyone on board still has the knowledge of how to do this."

"We can get a lot of information out of the manuals," Evelle said.

"Yes, but it's not as simple as it sounds. Docking the larger ships is a very delicate operation, and no one would want to do it by themselves."

"Gerry used to work in the docks," Evelle said. "He and Yonta."

"Oh, fuck, talk about the least compatible pair in our group," Aliz said.

"No one likes Yonta," Evelle said. "She's a bitch. Gerry is particularly bad because he speaks up about everything. They're always sniping at each other when no one is watching. But that's normal, and they'll do the work, anyway."

"That's going to be a fun job with those two."

CHAPTER EIGHT

THE ATMOSPHERE in the control room of the docking hall was tense.

The room was not big. The crew had used all the holdfasts along the walls, and now everyone was trying to stop themselves bumping into everyone else. This space was really too small to contain all of them.

But the docking hall, on the other side of the barrier, was ready to be opened to space.

Yonta and Gerry had set in motion the mechanisms that had moved the walls aside to make as much room as possible.

Tina had given them the specifications of the ship, and Yonta had calculated that the *Alethia* would just fit.

Now it was time to test out the work. They only got one chance at this and had to hope that no emergencies developed during this delicate operation.

So they all waited in the control room, watching the screen that showed what was happening in the hall.

The lights on the docking door flickered. Very slowly, it opened.

The arms extended from their recesses on both sides of the door.

On the outside camera appeared the familiar shape of the *Alethia*, her trusted ship with her son and friends on board.

The arms reached for the outside of the ship.

"It's going to be tight," Yonta said, facing the controls.

Slowly, the arms attached onto the surface.

This took a long time, because they had to clean the surface so the pads obtained a firm grip. A ship was heavy and a sudden move could mean severe damage to both vessels.

Because the *Alethia* was not a military vessel, the *Manila*'s database didn't contain precise details of the dimensions, so this had to be calibrated on the fly.

Yonta was doing this, and Gerry helped her.

They had a bit of a disagreement about his reluctance to help earlier, when they were moving the walls in the hall aside, but fortunately, he had decided to cooperate. Somehow, word had gotten out there would be eggs on board the *Alethia*. Tina had no idea how he had heard this.

Tina was glad for his help, because no one else could do this kind of work.

"All right. Now for the big test." Yonta shut down the last calibration.

She swivelled her seat to a different control panel and set some parameters there.

Lights on the arms flashed. At first, it was hard even to tell they were moving.

"We are going to be here forever," Gisele said. "What if a pirate ship comes?"

"Where almost done," Yonta said.

But at that moment, a red light started blinking on the control panel.

Yonta checked her instruments. "It doesn't fit."

"What do you mean?" Tina said. They had made sure all the ship's outer measurements were correct.

"It should fit according to your manual, but my instrument calibration tells me the ship won't fit in the docking bay."

"It will fit through the door?"

"It should, but that is not the problem. We need to get the ship past this point here." She pointed.

"Where exactly is the problem?" Tina's heart was hammering. She didn't want this to fail, because if they did, they would be no way she could see the others, because they didn't have a docking tube that would allow her to be transferred to her own ship, and suddenly she had an insane desire to be with her son and her somewhat ragtag band of friends.

"This diameter here is too wide."

She showed Tina the schematic on her screen that showed a wire frame scan of her familiar ship, with a red line from the point of one of the habitat's arms to the other side. The corresponding diameter across the other arm was slightly shorter.

"Why is it uneven?" Tina asked.

Yonta shrugged. "I don't know. It's not my ship."

"It's meant to be symmetrical... unless one of the arms hasn't folded correctly."

Crap. She remembered that this was sometimes a problem, one she had intended to fix, but she had not deemed to be overly important.

"Can I talk to them?" she asked.

"Sure."

Tina turned to the communication console and put on the earpiece Yonta handed her.

"Finn, can you hear me?"

"Yes, I can. What is the issue?"

"It seems one of the habitat arms is not folded properly and the ship won't fit."

"Do you want me to re-fold it?"

"Have a look and see if there is something you can do."

They watched in tense silence for a bit. The image on the camera was quite grainy. It was hard to make out whether the arm was moving.

Then Finn said, "Is this better?"

Yonta said, "I'm not seeing any difference."

"What do you mean? I moved the habitat out and back in a bit."

"I saw no movement."

"Well, in that case, it looks like the thing is jammed."

Damn it, that would mean sending someone out there to fix it from the outside. Of course they should have done that at the station, but that was all very easy to say in hindsight.

"Do we have anyone who can do EVA repairs?" Tina said, looking around the cabin.

But she already knew they didn't. Finn could possibly do it, but he was engaged with the other craft, and she couldn't expect any of the others to take the controls of this delicate operation.

She looked around the control room. "Is there a way we can make the opening bigger?"

Yonta shook her head. "What do you think? This is not a cargo vessel."

But Gerry pointed at the screen.

Yonta frowned at him. "What do you mean?"

"We could take that out." He pointed at an overhead arm that suspended the structure that held two fighter craft.

Yonta said, "And put it, where? I'm not happy to cut off access to the fighter craft."

"We can reposition them to the outside of the hull."

"That would mean having to EVA in order to access and resupply the craft."

"We have no one to fight battles with them, anyway."

"I guess... What do you think?" Yonta asked Aliz, who was watching from the bridge.

Aliz looked uneasy.

Gerry shrugged. "That's if you want to get this engineer on board."

"I think we should try it," Aliz said.

Tina knew that Aliz did want the engineer on board and was probably more worried about the state of the engine than she let on.

She asked about what needed to be done.

Yonta outlined the process, her voice terse.

First, they had to take the *Alethia* back out of the arms. Then they had to move the two fighters that were in the direct path to the outside of the hull.

There was external space for four fighters, each with an attachment post for refuelling and recharging.

Yonta said these were for in-battle refuels and only designed for short-term use.

"We might well lose the ships if we are forced to go through high-speed manoeuvres."

"How likely is it we'll do battle manoeuvres?" Aliz asked. "Those attachment points are quite sturdy. I'm willing to take the risk."

"You never know what will happen," Yonta said.

"Do we have people to fly the craft?" Zafira asked.

Yonta said, "It's not that I'm afraid of, but the damage the craft can do to the main hull when they come loose."

"Is there an alternative?"

Yonta shrugged. She clearly still didn't like it.

Aliz said, "I only want Tina and Evelle to touch those fighters."

Tina protested. "I have no experience with them either."

"No, but you have more experience flying than anyone else."

Tina knew she was right, but the responsibility lay heavy on her mind.

This was fast becoming a boring refrain: we know you're far from qualified, but we don't have anyone else to do it.

CHAPTER NINE

EVELLE TOOK Tina to the suiting area. Apparently it was not possible to fly the ships without wearing the elaborate pressure suit that pilots wore during proper sorties.

"I know it's a bother to dress up just to move the ships a small distance, but the suit connects with the ship's navigation, and you don't have full control of the ship when you're not wearing it," Evelle told her.

Well, so be it.

Just putting on the bottom half of the suit required assistance from another person because of the clips that needed to be done up and checked on the back, and because trying to do this in Zero-G made it hard to exert any kind of force. The legs of the inner suit were very snug and infuriating to put on.

Next came the top half of the suit. Especially the arms were a complex tangle of leads and patches.

Particular parts of the suit needed to line up with very specific parts of the body, because muscle movement steered the craft. Fortunately, Evelle knew how it worked. She explained how she and other people who worked in the flight support department had to take flight training in case of an emergency and had to keep up their accreditation.

"The arms and hands are for controlling the ship," Evelle said.

"Even the elbows?" Tina said as Evelle arranged the inner soft layer threaded through with sensors around her arms.

"Every part of the suit."

"Whatever happened to plain controls?"

"Nothing is plain about these babies. These craft are highly specialised killing machines."

"Just as well we aren't going to do any killing."

"If we did, I'd make you wear a nappy."

Tina remembered. She had been trained to fly the emergency evacuation vehicles, and nappies featured in that process, too. Like fighter craft, evacuation vehicles could pull a lot of Gs and people under that kind of stress were likely to have less control over their bodily functions.

After all that, the helmet was a relatively easy affair.

Tina could slip it on her head herself and only needed Evelle's assistance to make sure it was closed off properly. The leads from the helmet slotted into a pad on her arm, which lit up when she connected it to the battery pack. Evelle tested the receiver.

When that was all good, they went out into the hall.

The craft attached to the arms only looked small from a distance. From close up, they were much more impressive, sleek shapes of dark metal that would vanish against the background of space.

Evelle removed the engine covers while talking to Aliz on the bridge, going through the checks for all the craft's vitals while the data scrolled over the inner surface of her visor. She pointed to the ship furthest from the door that was to be Tina's.

Both craft were facing the large irising airlock door, so at least getting out was going to be straightforward, Tina hoped.

She was so awkward in the suit that she was beginning to feel very uncertain about this.

She pulled herself to the cabin and activated the control next to the door. The cover opened. Even through all the layers of the suit, she could hear the hydraulic engine's whine. She floated into the cabin, settled into the pilot's seat, and pressed the control that closed the cover again. Encased in her little cubicle, she found the attachment for the air hoses. The air inside her suit had become quite stuffy and hot, and now fresh air flowed over her sweaty face.

She was hot even before they were starting on this expedition.

Evelle was getting into the craft in front of Tina's, disappearing into the cabin.

Tina turned on the craft's receiver and listened to the instructions from Evelle about the basic operations of the ship. It was vastly more advanced than anything on board the *Alethia*.

Then, after what seemed like an eternity, the arms that held the craft in front of hers started to recede, leaving it floating in the air. A sideways force from the slight movement of the main ship pulled the craft to the side. Evelle corrected it with a brief engine burst.

The arms to Tina's craft receded as well, as indicated by lights flashing on the controls. Tina ran through the commands while Evelle instructed her.

The engine control panel lit up.

"Touch it once, and control will transfer to your gloves," Evelle said in her helmet.

Tina did, and she could feel the craft reacting through her fingertips.

"It's important not to make any sudden movements, especially not while we're still in the hall. And keep your arm entirely away from the firing controls."

"I'm not touching any of those."

"Watch the air hose. It's floating loose."

Evelle was right. Tina tucked the loop of hose into the bracket on the chair's armrest. "How did you know that, anyway? Can you see into here?"

"Yes, but that's standard practice. Your cabin camera is slaved to whichever craft leads the sortie. Are you ready?"

"Yes."

"Let's go then."

Evelle's craft moved ahead.

Tina followed carefully. The craft was very responsive.

The tiniest movement of her fingers would make it jerk. Curling her fingers increased the engine output. When she moved her hand, it changed the position of the craft up, down or sideways.

Evelle told her to hover in the middle of the open space in the hall to get a feel for the craft.

Evelle's craft had already started moving towards the open door.

Tina moved her hands forward and tipped her palms down.

When the craft shot forward, she quickly moved her palms up a bit more, and it slowed down. This was nothing like flying the *Alethia*. It was like playing a VR game.

That meant she was completely the wrong person to do this.

Rex would be excellent at this sort of thing.

Carefully, they both manoeuvred out of the dock into the opening in between the grappling arms and the *Alethia*.

From the outside, her faithful ship was looking its age, and showing off the fifteen years it had sat at Kelso Station unused.

But Tina was still proud of her ship. To be sure, all ships acquired this weatherbeaten exterior when they spent any time in space.

They moved away from the entrance and around the side of

the ship. Out here, the size of the Starfighter *Manila* became apparent. The ship was like a huge cigar, with the habitat built in a blocky attachment that sat in front of the particle acceleration chamber. It looked dark and solid, with the outside of the ship entirely encased in layers of shielding and no frippery like windows or viewing ports as would be present on civilian ships.

The attachment points and refuelling stations were directly ahead on the hull, not far away, Evelle said.

Indeed, it was only a short flight before Evelle slowed down to match her movement with the ship.

"I can't see anywhere for the ships to hang onto," Tina said.

"Wait and see," Evelle said. "I'm going down first. See the line of yellow dots?"

Yes, Tina saw them. There were four, quite a distance apart.

Evelle approached the furthest one.

A door opened on the hull and a pair of mechanical arms unfolded from the recess inside, with the blinking of little lights. Well, that was certainly very fancy.

Evelle made sure she shared all the commands for Tina to give to the arms when she approached the next yellow spot. It involved giving the handshake operation a code so the main ship could recognise her.

"You do not want to be seen as an enemy," Evelle said, and she laughed.

Tina was sure if that happened, it would be no laughing matter.

Evelle opened the canopy to her craft and guided Tina, watching while hanging onto a handrail that ran over the hull of the cover. She had already attached the cable from her tether to the railing.

The attachment procedure was not that hard. The automatic arms did most of the work.

They made sure both craft were secured, powered down and closed up.

Phew, the expedition was completed.

They made their way back via a clearly marked handhold trail over the outside of the ship to the airlock that led to the maintenance end of the docking hall. This area was still pressurised, even if the main hall was not.

Now that the delicate task was done, Tina felt more relaxed and could look around. The light from the system's distant star cast a pale glow over the side of the ship that made clear, crisp shadows. The auxiliary engine outlets—for steering the ship—protruding from the hull looked like big barnacles on the side of the dark matte surface of the spongy material that formed the outer layer of the protective shield.

Beyond that, the cluster of bigger specks against the black sky was the nearby asteroid field. They were too far away to spot the pirate ships that they knew were hiding there.

Space was dangerous.

When Tina and Evelle came to the airlock, they found the door stood open.

That was strange.

"Did someone go outside and leave it like that?" Tina asked. She didn't remember that anyone had gone outside.

"I don't think so. Anyway, in that case, it should have closed by itself," Evelle said. "That's what normally happens."

Evelle pressed a button on the panel next to the door.

The door started to close. Then she pressed it again, and it opened again. At least it still worked. Maybe Aliz had opened the airlock remotely, knowing they were going to use it. But still, it didn't sit well with Tina. It seemed like sloppy safety not to have an air lock properly closed.

They both squeezed into the cubicle. The light came on, and the outer door shut.

But after they had waited a while, Tina realised nothing was happening. There was no air hissing into the airlock.

"Why doesn't it work?" Tina asked.

"I don't know." Evelle's voice sounded worried.

Evelle asked Aliz, "Is there some sort of malfunction with this airlock?"

"Not that I can see. Ask Yonta."

Yonta said, "No, there is nothing wrong. Everything is working normally."

Even when the question had been completely legitimate, Yonta still managed to sound peeved.

They waited a bit longer, but nothing happened. Clearly, whatever was wrong didn't register with the control room.

"We will just have to find another airlock," Evelle said.

"Let's do that, then."

EVA protocol was to always have enough air in their tanks just for this reason.

Tina notified Aliz of their plans.

But just as Evelle was about to open the outer door again, air started hissing into the cubicle.

Tina said, "Scratch that. It's working again."

"Good," Aliz said. She sounded relieved.

They waited until the pressure had equalised, and then Evelle opened the inner door.

A widening shaft of light from inside the maintenance hall came into the cubicle—

A loud *thoomp* shook the air.

Tina was slammed against the back wall. A deafening whistle of air rushed past her.

An alarm started blaring in the hall.

A loud mechanical voice announced, "There is a breach in the hull. Repeat a breach in the hull. Repeat..." Over and over again.

The noise of the air screaming past Tina was so strong that it was hard to hear anything else. Evelle was yelling, and Tina tried to pull herself free, but she was stuck against the opening. She could only hope the door wouldn't open any further because she'd already taken off her tether.

With Evelle's help, she managed to roll off the opening far enough that Evelle could manually shut the door. The whistling of air stopped.

They had to wait until the pressure in the maintenance hall had equalised before the mechanical voice finally shut up.

"What the hell was that?" Aliz asked in Tina's helmet.

"I don't know why, but both airlock doors started to open at the same time."

"That's impossible."

CHAPTER TEN

———————————

TINA AND EVELLE made their way to the suiting area.

When taking off the cumbersome suit, Tina's hands trembled so much that she could barely get the helmet off, let alone the rest of the suit.

"Are you all right?" Evelle said.

"I think so." Tina's voice sounded insecure to her ears.

She managed to peel off the suit and the inner layer, which was clammy with sweat. She shivered with the sudden cold air over her skin.

Concern hovered over Evelle's face. "Look, you've got a red mark on your back."

Tina turned around where she pointed, and saw it too, a long shape over her side, where she had been sucked into the opening. It had bruised even through the suit.

"That will probably be a nice bruise tomorrow," she said, forcing herself to sound cheerful.

She smiled, but it felt forced even to her.

"It's okay to say that your shaken," Evelle said. "I would feel shaken, too."

"I am," Tina said, feeling the pressure ooze off her.

She was too old for this type of shit.

"We have to find out why this happened," Aliz said in her earpiece.

"Can you see any kind of malfunction reported up there?" Evelle asked.

"No, I can't. The records for the air lock are all normal."

"You can operate it from the cabin?" Tina asked, her mouth stiff.

"I can operate everything from here, but only if someone asks me to do it."

Then Evelle said, "There is an override in the maintenance hall."

"That is true, maybe that has malfunctioned."

Evelle and Tina packed up their suits, put their overalls back on, and went to the maintenance hall's control room.

Most of the other women were preparing for the arrival of the *Alethia* in the dock. They needed to be ready to shut the big doors and re-pressurise the hall. They needed to connect the ship's feeder leads.

When Tina and Evelle came into the control room, they found only Gerry in the room.

He glanced at them and quickly moved something off the screen in front of him.

"Where is Yonta?" Evelle asked.

"She had to do something," Gerry said. "She asked me to look after the controls."

Evelle gave Tina a suspicious glance.

"Did you see anything unusual?" Evelle asked. "We were just almost sucked out of a malfunctioning airlock."

"Oh, was that what the alarm was about?"

Tina frowned. This guy was supposed to work in this hall? What sort of monkeys did the Force employ these days?

Evelle said, "You said Yonta asked you to look after the controls?"

"Well, yes... but it's boring, so I was playing a game... you know."

"Where is Yonta?"

He shrugged. "She had to check something."

Tina and Evelle left the room.

"Yonta wouldn't give him the controls," Evelle said when they were far enough so he couldn't hear her. "She thinks he's lazy and wouldn't trust her enemy's life in Gerry's hands."

"Then what? They were in here together. You don't think he..." But she didn't speak that thought out loud.

No, that was ridiculous.

She was sure there was a logical explanation for the malfunction, only now would be a good time to reveal what that explanation was.

They looked for Yonta and finally found her looking into the open cover of a maintenance panel.

"Did anything malfunction?" Tina asked.

"Did I say that? I'm just getting ready to connect the air supply to your ship's umbilicals. It's much bigger than anything we usually have in here, so we need a lot more air."

Tina clenched her jaw. Yonta didn't make it easy for people to communicate honestly with her. She always assumed that everyone was accusing her.

"I was only asking because I nearly got sucked out the airlock when both doors opened at the same time. Didn't you hear the alarm?"

"If it was the one in the main hall, I won't hear it in this part." She showed no horrified reaction, and that disturbed Tina as well.

"Then why was Gerry in the control room? He said you needed to do something and asked him to sit in the hub."

"I didn't ask him. Between you and me, there are a lot of people I'd ask before I'd ask him. As soon as you two left, I sent everyone to prepare for the next phase of the docking."

"But who was looking after the hub?"

"No one needs to look after it. I carry the controls on here." She held up her pad.

"But you didn't hear the alarm go off with the hull breach?"

Now Yonta frowned at her.

She brought the pad to life by holding it up to her face. She flicked through a few pages before she froze.

"Shit. Why didn't you tell me about this?" Now her voice was angry.

"That was a bit hard. I was stuck against the airlock door that wouldn't shut."

"We did try to contact you before it happened," Evelle said. "You said that everything was working normally. Were you actually in the control room when you said that?"

Yonta breathed in deeply. In her eyes, Tina saw that she had not been in the control room, and realised she should have been, and maybe Gerry had been in there, although he shouldn't have been. But Yonta shouldn't have left that room. She was out of people she could blame.

Yonta's expression went hard. "I'll deal with this later, *after* I've had a word with Gerry."

She put her pad in her pocket, turned around and pushed herself out the door.

Evelle met Tina's eyes. She said, "We don't need pirates to kill us. We'll soon be killing each other."

"Do we need to keep an eye on them?"

"That's probably a good idea. Murders are messy."

Evelle was joking, but Tina wasn't sure that she wasn't also serious.

Tina and Evelle followed Yonta at a slower pace through the corridors of the ship. All of a sudden, its vast emptiness depressed her.

They could hear the voices long before they reached the

control room: Yonta tearing into Gerry and Gerry shouting back at her.

At training, before recruits took their first mission, they were taught how to handle conflict, to call the supervisor, to moderate language and things like that. It sounded like this training had totally gone out the window.

When they rounded the corner to the control room, there was a loud bang, and Gerry flew from the room.

"What was that?" Evelle asked.

Tina didn't like how her voice sounded panicked. She didn't think anyone had weapons on board the ship, but of course you could never be sure.

They entered the room, where Yonta was at the controls. Everything looked normal, and for a moment Tina felt like she had panicked for nothing, and was even getting angry about it, until she saw Yonta's flaring nostrils.

"What did he do?" Evelle asked.

"He messed up all the systems." Yonta's voice trembled with anger.

"But why would he do that?"

"He says he wanted to help, but he's just trying to be a pain in the butt to me. He's always been a little creep. He fancies himself as better at my job than I am. You would think that he would actually show that he is better at it."

Evelle looked at the door. "Where did he go?"

"I don't know. I hope as far away as possible."

Evelle met Tina's eyes, jerking her head at the door.

They left the control room.

"We have to find him," Evelle said, her voice low.

Tina agreed. She had no idea what had just happened in that room, and who had threatened whom, and where that bang had come from.

But they had the *Alethia* to bring into the dock first. Although she wondered what Finn would make of this situation. It was really a pity that the *Manila* had no soft-docking facilities. She knew she would not leave Evelle alone in this big ship with too few crew, but tying up her only way of escape with the fate of the *Manila* seemed a step too far in the other direction.

Reconfiguring the hall was a lot of work, more because Gerry wasn't there to assist them with the one thing he knew how to do well.

The storage wall that held the remaining fighters needed to be moved back. This could be done remotely without entering the hall, but the loosening of the wall and moving it back needed to be coordinated with precision.

They moved the wall back as far as it would go while allowing the remaining fighter craft room to get out if necessary.

It was a very slow process.

Finally, they declared everything ready for another try.

Then Aliz spoke to Finn, giving him instructions. Tina watched with tenseness as the grappling arms moved again and her beloved ship came closer to the opening. First she could only see it on the screen, and then through the viewport in the door to the control centre.

First it went light in the hall as the light from outside reflected off the metal surface into the docking bay, and then it grew very dark as the ship entered the opening and blocked the light from outside. Very slowly, with blinking lights and soft beeping alarms, the ship moved inside. Then the docking hall's arms extended and took the ship in its embrace.

The air lock door closed and with a soft shudder the hall started filling up with air.

"Done," Aliz said.

Tina breathed out a sigh of relief. That ship was her entire life now, no matter that it looked a little battered and in need of a coat of paint, no matter that one of the arms wouldn't fold up properly.

Aliz told Finn to shut down engine operations.

With a soft whine, the main engine powered down completely, leaving only the low hum of the steering engines. They would continue running for a while to cool down the engine chamber.

The lights came on, and then a hiss signalled that the door into the hall unlocked and it was safe to go in.

Slowly, the door to the *Alethia* opened.

A figure appeared in the doorway, back-lit by the glow from the cabin.

The person floated out into the hall.

It was Finn.

CHAPTER ELEVEN

TINA COULDN'T BELIEVE how glad she was to see him. She made her way across the hall.

"Finn!"

She hugged him tightly, breathing the familiar smell from inside her ship.

He kind of awkwardly held her.

"I didn't think you two were that close," a male voice said. It was a familiar voice, but yet...

Rex had grown even more than she had imagined. What was more, his harness expertly dealt with weightlessness, and he didn't appear as clumsy as everyone else.

"Did you miss me, too?"

Tina hugged him, a very hard hug of plastic panels and metal.

She touched his face, feeling the rasp of stubble on his chin. Her son was a man, and no longer a boy.

Thor and Jens also came out, followed by Rasa. Everyone was smiling. Despite all their troubles, the world suddenly looked brighter.

"I have to have a look inside the ship," Tina said.

She wasn't sure why. She just wanted to see the familiar cabin that had been her home.

She pushed off and floated into the entry. Weightlessness had dislodged a certain number of things: a cup, a screwdriver, someone's shirt, but no more than usual. Facing with having to fold the habitat, they would have given removing important items out of the habitat priority over securing loose bits and pieces.

The cabin was a bit messy and worn, but it was home. Even the smell of it was familiar. How had she missed her ship.

But then she noticed an odd screeching sound.

"What's that noise?"

"Oh, the geese have been carrying on a bit," Rex said.

"It's not a sound I've heard them make before."

"You'll be surprised when you see them."

"Can I?" That didn't sound good.

Rex floated ahead of her to the two storage rooms in the short passage behind the control room.

He opened the door to the storage room where the cage for the geese stood.

But Tina could barely see the cage for the growth of prickly fronds.

"Holy crap. Have the cactuses grown that much?"

It was not the usual type of growth either, with branches breaking out in unfamiliar leaves with green and white patterns. The tips of the fronds were covered in pink berry-like growths. Tina had never seen the cactuses produce those, either.

The geese had changed almost unrecognisably from the white birds with yellow beaks that Tina had last seen.

Most birds had grown feathers of varying colours: brown, grey, black, even green and red like a parrot. Some feathers were curly or fine and fluffy, like hair.

A couple of birds had feathers on their feet and on the membranes between their toes.

One had grown a curved beak like a parrot. It was screeching like a parrot, too.

"What has happened to the geese?" Tina asked Rex.

"I don't know. They really liked the cactuses, and they kept escaping. We couldn't always catch them quickly. They've gotten very good at getting out of the cage."

Obviously.

"Try to keep them locked up, please. We're now on board a very large warship, and I don't want to have the responsibility for them getting into secret military installations. I don't want anyone to see these animals."

"Why not? They're pretty," Rasa said.

"Yeah, but people would start asking questions we can't answer, and you never want to give a military officer a reason to ask a question, especially one you can't answer."

Finn was nodding. He knew exactly what she was talking about.

They shut the door and returned to the main cabin.

Tina had an insane desire to slip into the pilot seat, take the craft and leave, but of course it was far too late for that, and she had already decided she couldn't leave Evelle, anyway.

"Seriously, mum, is there no rotating habitat in this place?" Rex asked.

"This is a fighter ship, so no."

"Does that mean we've got to float around like this all the time?" Rasa said.

"All the time," Tina confirmed. "You'll find that the ship is designed for it."

"They must spend a lot of time at the gym," Rex said.

"I'm sure they do."

Rasa pulled a face.

Rex smiled at her.

Rasa had stayed with Rex all the time, and Tina was once again wondering about what went on between the two of them.

"There don't seem to be too many people inside this ship," Jens said.

"That was why we needed you. They have technical problems. The pilot thinks the main engine may be damaged because of overheating."

"Just how many are there on board?" Finn asked.

"Sixteen."

"Is that all? A ship like this needs fifty people just to fly it safely."

Tina sighed. "Sixteen was all we could rescue."

"Crap. Just between you and me, make sure we don't get trapped here. This place feels like a flying sarcophagus."

By taking the *Alethia* into the stricken fighter, Tina might have risked all of them.

"Come, and you can meet the rest of the crew."

Almost everyone except Aliz had congregated outside the entrance.

Several people gasped when Rex came out of the craft.

"They've got a cyborg," someone whispered.

"This is my son, Rex," Tina said. "He wears a walking harness that's extremely useful and powerful. Inside the harness is a human boy. He is usually friendly, and you can talk to him like a normal person."

Rex was studying the crew. "Mum, which one is she?"

"That one over there. Evelle, meet your brother."

Evelle came closer, a little gingerly and unsure. She was so much smaller than Rex, with her very slight pixie-like build. She had to look up at him. He towered over her.

"Well," she said, looking him up and down. "Look at that. Mum said you were much younger than me."

"I'm fifteen."

Evelle didn't say that she was twenty-nine. Rex knew that anyway.

"You're so big," she said.

"When we are adults, size doesn't matter."

"Your name is Rex?"

"Yep."

"I'm Evelle."

"Yes. Mum told me."

There was a super-awkward silence.

Then Rex said, "Is this your ship?"

"I'm part of the crew, yeah."

"What is your job?"

"I'm normally navigator, but I've been promoted to second pilot."

"Wow. Did you know I can fly this ship—in the simulator?"

"Yeah, sure." She laughed.

"I mean—it's a game we play, Jens and I."

"You play games a lot?"

"Not all the time. I work, too. I can do all kinds of computer repairs with my mate Jens here."

He looked at Jens, who was admiring the docking hall and especially the fighter craft that were hanging on the side. Tina hoped Evelle didn't realise that "repairs" was a euphemism for hacking into systems.

"Are those the new dragon fighters?" Jens asked Evelle.

She seemed taken aback. "Yes, they are. What do you know about them?"

"I read the release papers. We play games, you know, flying the craft virtually."

"Not these ones. The details are secret."

"Yes, these ones. The simulator is semi legal. The model we use was adapted from the Wasp fighters who formed the basis of the design of the Dragon series. The most common one is the Dragon-1, but these are Dragon-3 and almost no one has seen them, but people are selling online models that have all the specs on the black market for thousands."

"To make games," Evelle said, her tone flat.

"What else would we do with it?"

"Uh, fight wars?"

"That's what we do, except we don't kill anyone."

"And you really reckon you could fly one of these?" She sounded like she didn't believe that for one second.

"Only if the model is right."

"The models Jens has are amazing," Rex said, barging into this strange conversation. "You can see everything on the entire ship. The game also has a hall that looks exactly like this. Some versions of the ship have artificial gravity."

"Only when they're docked at a station," Jens said.

Rex's eyes widened. "Of course. Now I see. I'd been wondering about that. It seemed sloppy for the designers to have gravity in one frame and none in another."

Jens and Evelle were still eyeing each other. Evelle's face carried a suspicious expression, and Tina didn't think Jens was as innocent as he looked.

Tina's initial feeling about him and Rex had been right.

The crew were wondering who they had left on board to fly these craft, but even military pilots took a lot of virtual training before they ever set foot inside an actual ship. Potentially, Jens and Rex only needed a few practical lessons to become relatively proficient with them, especially the part that required chasing down and shooting other craft. That was something to keep in the back of her mind.

If necessary.

Only in the utmost emergency.

Someone in the group said that it was time for dinner, and most people started making their way out of the hall.

But before Tina could go after them, Finn motioned for her to stay back. His face carried a concerned expression.

CHAPTER TWELVE

———————

FINN TOOK Tina back inside the cabin of the ship while the others continued to the kitchen.

"Why did it take so long to dock the ship after you moved us back out?" he asked, his voice low and tone urgent. "Is anything wrong?"

Tina sighed. "Where do I begin? Nothing is 'wrong' in so many words, but…"

"Have you been coping all right in here?" Finn said.

"Up to a point," Tina said. She didn't quite realise how much she had missed Finn and his steady judgement. Even if they also disagreed at times.

"Only a bit?"

"Things have been quite tense on board. We don't have enough people to operate the ship safely, and people have been bickering."

"Even more than aboard the *Alethia*?"

Tina chuckled, but the feeling of mirth soon died down. "I mean serious bickering. Not clowning around. Do you know what happened in that time that we tried to get you in and we had to take the ships out to make space for the *Alethia*?"

Tina explained to him and a few sentences.

"Holy shit," he said. "You could have been sucked into space."

Tina nodded.

And then he said nothing for a while.

"Listening back to it, I'm even frightened myself," Tina said. "I'm sorry about bringing you to this ship." She was silent for a while. "Also, I can't just let these women float aimlessly out here while we take the *Alethia* to go to Olympus. I'm no longer convinced going to Olympus is the best option, anyway."

Tina then explained to him how they had rescued the men at Aurora Station, how they had been asleep in cubicles, and how she was afraid they might already be infected.

She finished with, "At least that's my conclusion about what the pirates were doing in the labs: actively turning people into more pirates."

"There is talk that the infection makes you live longer and have more strength."

"If you survive the initial process, and anyway, you end up looking like a toad."

"Does that matter if everyone else looks like a toad, too?"

Tina gave a small chuckle, because Finn could see the humour. His problem was that being part of an influential family had also made him suspicious and paranoid, but if he'd grown up in a normal family, he would definitely be a great guy.

She sighed.

"The problem with the *Manila* is that the crew is a unit and the women care about their colleagues, and they even want to go back to the station to rescue the rest of the crew."

Finn nodded. "That's what the crew on my ship the *Stavanger* would have done. You spend so much time with each other, that even the people you know and hate are better than the ones you don't know."

"I'm not sure going back is a good idea. But on the other hand, we desperately need crew."

"Are there any other Federacy ships in the area? I thought I saw some indistinct blips on the radar when we were waiting for you out there and I was scrolling through screens looking for you."

"Apparently they're in hiding, waiting to set a trap for the pirate fleet, and wouldn't be in the capacity to help us, anyway."

"Is the pilot still in contact with their command? It seems a funny question, but the *Stavanger* where I served was a highly autonomous ship. As an engineer, I sometimes got to see communication from the captain to the upper command at Olympus. We weren't supposed to see it, but sometimes I needed to do something that allowed me to see it, anyway. These ships go for months without hearing from Olympus, or reporting their position."

"The pilot must have had contact. The ship was part of a fleet."

"You're not sure?"

Tina shrugged. "Aliz has told me, but I haven't actually seen any communication. At any rate, she told me the next ship is quite a distance away, and also they're reluctant to come this way for fear of being ambushed again. It appears they also lost crew. The crew of the *Manila* don't have any orders beyond not to let the ship fall into the hands of others. That's precisely what happened, so the ship crew is not keen to angle for orders, since those orders are likely to contain a castigation for surrendering the ship to pirates."

"How did that happen?"

"No idea. It seems to be a sore point. None of the crew have spoken much about it. Those who were on the bridge at the time of capture are not in our group."

Tina remembered what Rae had said about corruption

within the crew and the fact that there might still be people on board with ulterior motives.

Finn sniffed. "Hmmm, I'm guessing that even if they can re-establish communication, the upper command will be hesitant to rely on this ship because it has been in pirate hands. They are unsure what devices the pirates might have installed in the communication system, and they don't want the ship to rejoin the rest of the fleet, because of what the pirates might find out."

That was also true and something that Aliz would realise, but might come as a shock to some others. The ship was both an asset and a risk to the Federacy Force.

She said, "So, what can we do? Will we fix the *Manila's* engine and then take the *Alethia* on to Olympus?"

"I just want to warn you that things there are not as you assume," he said. "And everyone around here already thinks very little of the Federacy Assembly."

"What do you mean?"

His face was full of concern, an expression she didn't like.

"While we were waiting for you, I've been in contact with the Assembly, and it's not all rosy over there."

"In contact with your family over there?"

"With them, and a few others. Rex managed to get into this amazing program, which lets you visit the Assembly in real time and listen to what is going on there. I'll show you some of it."

He gave Tina a pair of VR goggles, and she put them on, while hanging onto the navigator seat.

After a few flashes of menus across her vision, a scene played in front of Tina's eyes.

She stood at the gallery of a large hall, and beneath her, people sat on semicircular rows of benches.

Those benches stood in groups, where the front row of people were listening and taking part in the debate, and in the rows behind them sat people at work stations who were recording, reading on screens and communicating with people outside the hall.

She had never been to the Federacy Assembly at Olympus, but she had seen these types of images many times.

The Federacy's executive council sat at the main desk at the far end of the room. She recognised the faces of several long serving counsellors.

On the floor of the hall, behind a dais, stood a man who was vaguely familiar to Tina. His face was red as he shouted into the microphone.

"And so do you think, senators, that we should allow this to happen? That we should allow these people to go hungry and deny them any form of help? They are not affected by this condition of their own volition. Many of them have demanded our help. They asked for assistance, and what have we done? We've sent armies. Armies can't do anything against the pirate scourge, anyway. When these pirates fight, they fight well. Our military fleets have been defeated, most of them are so scattered that they are no longer effective. The Force won't tell us this, but that's what I'm hearing in their words. We need to approach this differently."

A barrage of shouts erupted from the floor.

A man further up in the gallery yelled, "We should never give in to these criminals. That's what they are."

"Yes. Do you suggest we talk to them? That will only embolden them."

"Calm down everyone," the chairwoman said, her voice dry. "The delegate from Peris City can make his point."

Tina realised why she recognised the man and also now recognised him as one of the most obnoxious financiers in Peris City. Since when had they gained so much power?

The man continued, "My argument remains, that many

people did not choose to catch this infection that transforms them into pirates and therefore they deserve our help. We need to reach out to them. That was the most important point I wanted to make." He made a show of sitting down again, while the hall broke out into a shouting match.

From far off, Finn's voice said, "Do you see? They're not really interested in fighting the pirates."

Tina took off the goggles and looked into Finn's face, pale in the semidarkness of the control cabin. In the background, the geese were honking at each other.

Tina said, "They want to negotiate with the pirates? You can't negotiate with them. They're mentally incapable."

"But he is also right that they didn't choose to become affected like this."

"That's true, but that still doesn't mean that you can negotiate with pirates. They are not sensible and can't understand reason. All they want is to win. Violently, if they can. And they don't care about the suffering they cause. They've ceased to be normal humans."

That had become very clear in her meeting with Artan. And she shuddered at the thought that she could have prevented this if only fifteen years ago, she had shut down the skewed priorities of those in charge of Project Charon, those who wanted to make money out of the rift material against her scientific advice.

Finn nodded, meeting her eyes. "I know they're not human, but this is what's happening in the Assembly. People think they need to help the pirates because they are to be pitied. My family also confirms this. Even if you think little of my family, there is one thing they are familiar with: how to sell things. My family expressed their great frustration that they can't negotiate any commercial deals with these pirates, because they lie and cheat."

"I thought your family wanted to keep that distinction to themselves."

"And yes, well, they don't like having competition."

At any other time that would have been a joke, but the situation was too serious.

Tina said, "So you're saying the Assembly has become compromised?"

"There is definitely that possibility, whether by design or not."

"What do you mean?" Tina felt cold.

"I mean, these delegates may not realise that calling for negotiations will end up playing into the hands of the pirates."

"I see." Tina breathed out. For a moment, her thoughts had gone in directions that scared her deeply. For example, that the pirate army was just a ruse hiding a deeper plot. One that involved distracting the Assembly and Force with an army, while something worse was going on... like what? She had no idea.

Finn sighed. "Anyway, I don't think there is much point in going to the Assembly. We'll just hand them information they'll use against us."

"Then what are we supposed to do?"

"I don't know. I truly don't know. Knowing what to do with my life has never been my strong suit."

"You have a point there."

A kind of hopeless silence followed. Tina had no further suggestions, because the issues were all so big. It had seemed simple: go to Olympus and deliver her material, and go back to her shop and pretend nothing happened.

Why had she ever believed things would be so simple?

Finn said, "I understand you're the boss here."

Tina sighed. "I'm not sure. They're military women and they want a leader and orders they can follow. I was through with the concept of orders when I left the Force. Was never much good at following them, either. We need help. But there isn't anyone in the system who can help us. No other military ships, no allies we can trust, not on the station, or in space."

"There's the scientists," Finn said.

"You mean Arkady and his friends on Aurora? They're dealing with their own problems. I don't think they can or want to help us. Because otherwise they would have told us so."

"I think you'd be surprised," Finn said. "Also, you're forgetting the Freerangers."

"The Freerangers? They are just a handful of independent eccentric merchants who got confused with what belongs under the 'pirate' tag."

"They're a little more than that. When Rasa and I went back to the station, we came into contact with some of them."

"So did we, when we were there. I remember those people in their funny blue and red robes."

"I agree, they look quaint, but once you talk to them, there is a lot more to their shipworlds."

"How so?"

"Well, for one, they all successfully operate at least one ship per group, most likely more. They know about fleet operations, about transfers between ships, about hiding out in an asteroid field, about avoiding the major travel routes. Sometimes they may do this for reasons we don't agree with, but that doesn't mean they're not skilled."

"What made you all full of respect for these people all of a sudden?"

"You should listen to how they speak with each other."

"Like what?"

Finn pulled out his communication device. He swiped across the screen to turn it on.

"It probably won't work on here, but I'll give it a try."

Tina recognised the logo of the *Alethia*'s operating system on the screen.

"You rigged it so that you can control the ship from that thing?"

"It was Jens' idea. I need to sleep sometimes, and I let the others sit at the controls. Sometimes the autopilot would bring up a question. I got sick of getting out of bed in order to look at it and answer it."

He cycled through a few screens and then pressed a button.

A voice came out of the device. It was a male voice, and a second male voice replied. Tina picked up a handful of words but couldn't understand most of the conversation between the two men.

"What are they saying?"

"That's just it. They always speak in code, and only another Freeranger will understand what it means, because apparently the meaning of the words changes all the time. They know you can't hide in space, so they developed a thing they call hiding in plain sight. Make sure no one knows what you're talking about, then they can listen all they want."

"And this makes them suitable to help us?"

"You have to admit it's useful. It's not their only skill. They are very accomplished pilots."

"But their ships are rust buckets. "

"That makes it even more interesting. They can do precision operations, even though their ships are not modern. They're also extremely familiar with this entire area. And they're in contact with a lot of other people who can help, and they know who to stay away from as well. Most importantly, there are a lot of them, and they know about spaceships. About operating them, about fixing them, about towing them."

"And do you can get in contact with these people?"

"As I said, I met a couple when we went back to the station. It was the family that wears blue. There are eighty-two of them, and they operate four ships, which are all in this area. They include engineers and pilots. They're also loaded up with food from the stores of the *Manila*."

"That reminds me, we better bring those supplies to the galley. Margot was most put out about the lack of choice left in her storage cabinets."

CHAPTER THIRTEEN

THEY MADE their way to the mess hall, which had become a gathering place.

Margot and Gisele were busy preparing something to eat that even smelled like food. Tina hadn't realised how hungry she was.

"It's not much," Margot said, bringing a tray with covered bowls. "The supplies onboard are quite limited."

Cally lifted one side of the lid and pulled a face. "Not rice again."

"Well, if you want curry to go with your fake rice, that's all we've got in our kitchen," Rex said.

"So that's where it all went," Margot said.

"We can bring some of it back," Tina said, but as she said this, she realised that if they returned a significant proportion of the current supplies of the *Alethia*, their own capability to leave would be in danger.

Tina started eating, but, like some others, like Miriam, kept looking at the door. Gerry had not yet come in, and no one had seen him since the argument between him and Yonta.

But slowly the ice broke between the two groups, and people started talking.

Thor found that he and Rae shared a period of service, and he spent most of dinner speaking to her, while Finn briefed Tina on what had happened since they had parted and how he had gone back to the station to pick up Thor, Jens and Rex.

"It was easy, really," he said. "We were still registered as commercial ship and no one questioned us. There were a lot of ships coming back, because many people at the station still like to do business with the pirates."

"Yeah," she said. "That's the trouble, the pirates pay money for things. If ever I was going to lead a revolution, it would be a revolution through business. Give people an opportunity to earn a lot of money for themselves and they'll follow you into a black hole."

"Yeah." He nodded and looked down at his hands. "I'm afraid we've all played a part in the spread of the pirate disease throughout settled space. I probably more than anyone. My family gave them lots of money early on."

Someone—Tina didn't see who—remarked that Gerry still hadn't turned up.

This made everyone stop talking.

"Well, he better turn up soon," Margot said. "That's if he wants something to eat."

"Someone should find him," Miriam said. "He'll be hungry."

Yonta rolled her eyes. "Seriously? We don't need to babysit him. If he wants food, he knows where it is. I'm done with making excuses for him. If he wants to be a dickhead, he can go be a dickhead."

"He may not be well," Zafira said. "All the men are still recovering."

Tina glanced at the remaining two men, but both didn't seem to have any problem with the statement.

In fact, Vito was hanging onto the holdfast bar next to Miriam. His face carried a dreamy expression.

"I agree he may need medical attention," Rae said. "I think we should try to find him. If he's in his cabin asleep, then that's good to know, too."

"He isn't in his cabin," Miriam said.

"We should definitely check," Tina said.

Because there were thousands of ways someone with an ill mind could damage the ship, and their chances of survival, if he had flipped out.

Most people in the group agreed that someone should check out if he was all right and bring him dinner.

They divided into groups to search the ship.

Tina paired up with Rex and Finn, who didn't seem to appreciate her worry. Especially Rex enjoyed seeing the parts of the ship that would never be visible to the public.

Finn said he had worked with similar ships and that he'd speak with Aliz about what she wanted checked out.

To Tina, the vast emptiness of the ship was becoming ever more depressing. The ship made creaking and groaning noises you normally couldn't hear over the sounds made by people. You could never hear fluids bubble through the supply lines, or the ticking of the pipes as they expanded and contracted.

They wandered from empty room to empty room. Some part of Tina's over-active imagination expected Gerry to come out with an axe with every corner they turned.

But Gerry remained elusive.

When they gathered back in the mess, none of the other groups had found a trace of Gerry either.

Not everyone had heard the story of why Gerry was missing. Yes, they were aware he'd had an argument with Yonta, but didn't know about the mishap with the airlock door that nearly resulted in Tina getting sucked into space and the fact that Yonta had not been at the controls when that happened.

"If it is really Gerry's doing, and we can prove it, he will be off to the brig," Cally said.

A few others agreed.

"But we don't know and can't prove it," Tina said. "We can't be sure about what happened."

She felt very conflicted about Gerry. Without him, there was no way they could have gotten the *Alethia* inside the dock, but it wasn't the first time she'd wondered if the men were really as normal as they appeared. And she was afraid to speak about it, especially with the other men present.

"People will find out what happened," Zafira said, glaring at Vito, who still didn't react, and that lack of reaction disturbed Tina more than anything.

"I can't see how 'people' can know," Lisette said, her voice prim. "I don't like making assumptions."

"Well, we can simply ask," Zafira said. "And failing that, we can watch the recordings of the security cameras."

"I don't know what you're getting at," Miriam said. "Yes, my Vito is friends with Gerry. He has a temper, but I don't understand why you all link the incident with the airlock door to him. Gerry is a good man. But you know, if you think he's so evil, why don't you search his cabin? Just make sure to be done with this when you find nothing. Because you will find nothing. They're just recovering from what those dreadful pirates put them through. Isn't it?"

She turned to Vito, who merely nodded.

Tina didn't like the blank look in his eyes.

There really was no good time to voice her doubts, but she would have to talk about it at some point.

It was late, and everyone was cranky and tired. People announced they were going to bed.

That left Tina with having to sort out the sleeping arrangements. With the habitats folded and the geese occupying one of the two available rooms and the other taken up by various flotsam, the only place where the crew could sleep in the *Alethia* was in the main cabin, and it only contained one couch and a couple of anchor points for Zero-G sleeping bags, and those bags themselves were... well, that was a good question, wherever they were. At any rate, there was not enough space for everyone to sleep, so Tina arranged rooms and bedding for Finn and Thor.

Rasa had been quiet during dinner, but when Tina asked, she refused to sleep anywhere outside the ship.

Tina remembered how nervous Rasa had been when Tina first came to sell the ship. It had been Rasa's home, the sole point of certainty in her life, and officially becoming part of the crew hadn't changed that.

Rex said he also wanted to stay on board.

Yeah—right. This brought home another problem she needed to deal with.

Tina accompanied the two of them back to the docking hall. When they arrived at the craft, Rex was the first to go into the cabin.

Tina hesitated.

She didn't want to go where she was about to venture, but this was one of those rare chances, and if she didn't take it, next time it might be too late.

"Rasa, can I talk to you for a bit?" She jerked her head at a space in the shadow of one of the remaining fighter craft.

Rasa raised her eyebrows, but came with Tina.

They went far enough away to hopefully be out of earshot of Rex.

"I just want you to realise that if you're an adult and you're doing adult things, there can be adult consequences. You and Rex are both sixteen and—"

Rasa laughed.

"I don't know what you're thinking, but it's nothing like that. I like him. He's nice. I like helping him, but that's all. Besides, don't worry about me. See this?" She lifted her sleeve, displaying the dark tattoo Tina had noticed before. "This writing says Nephthys. It's ancient, from a place called Egypt. I looked it up once. Nephthys is a goddess of infertility. The station command at Kelso gives this to all girls after they've been 'helped'."

She smiled while she said this, but the words cut into Tina's heart.

Girls that had been 'helped', so they couldn't produce more impoverished children.

Well, she was glad she didn't have that talk with Rex, because, to be honest, who was she to deny him something he'd never thought he would have?

And chances were she was *still* wrong about what happened between the two of them when no one was looking.

But that was unlikely.

Tina Freeman, you're jealous.

Jealous of the rush of first love that she had wasted on men who didn't deserve it.

Was there a type of person capable of making you feel more like an idiot than a precocious teenage girl?

CHAPTER FOURTEEN

AFTER THAT EMBARRASSING EPISODE, Tina returned to her cabin. Work on the ship was going to start tomorrow morning. First, they would rest.

Rae was already in her hammock.

Tina took her shoes off, put them in the locker and strapped herself in the hammock. A control panel for the screen was next to the attachment point. She turned it on, half-expecting it not to work, but the Federacy logo jumped up.

"Ha, they still use the same arrow to show which way is up," she said.

"The entertainment choice probably hasn't changed much either."

"Yeah." Oh hell, yes, that memory came back to her. The Federacy found it necessary to vet entertainment on their ships, so any news that was not covered by the Force's own news service was late, shows were heavily biased towards the Federacy's point of view, and on a ship like this, the crew would have zero bandwidth for obtaining contraband shows.

"I read a lot," Rae said, in reply to Tina's unasked question. "Read and study."

"Have you been on the ship long?"

"About two years. Completed a whole extra degree in astrobiology in that time."

"You're kidding. That's my study field. We never had much bandwidth either at Project Charon, so I did electronics in my spare time. That was pretty handy for when I had to run a shop on Cayelle."

"A shop? Selling what?"

"Security gear. My family was always into selling things. They were agricultural settlers at Tirkala."

"Do you have much family still there?"

"Three brothers, some cousins and my mother. I haven't seen them for years. What about your family on Olympus?"

"I have a sister and my mother. My father died a few years ago."

"I'm sorry."

"Don't be. He had been ill for years. He never wanted to talk to me after I signed up."

This reminded Tina of her own fractured family. "I never saw my parents again after I signed up, either. Once I ended up at Project Charon, I wasn't allowed to go home."

"The Federacy Force are very good at separating people from their families, right?"

Tina shrugged. "It seems that for all of us who go into space, our family lives are kind of fucked up."

Rae chuckled. "You can say that again."

They were silent for a bit. Tina took off her clothes and wormed herself into the sleeping bag.

"You were suggesting yesterday that the ship fell into the hands of pirates because some people were taking grease money?"

"There is always someone taking grease money."

That didn't answer the question. "Do you have proof?"

"I don't have a death wish. Those who are compromised

cover their tracks well, and they don't hesitate to take action against those they perceive as whistleblowers. We can't really do anything unless we have hard proof and often not even then."

"Then why did you tell me yesterday?"

"I thought I should warn you." And after a short silence, she added, "I was told, not so long ago, that there used to be a brilliant scientist who worked for the Force, but when she discovered that other people in the project were dealing in illegal experimental material and she protested, those in power forced her to resign, leaving all of us to face the shame of our inaction. I want to make up for being complicit. I want to be brave."

Tina was going to say that she wasn't brave either when she realised she was the scientist in the story. Then she was going to say that she had achieved nothing, but she realised she had.

Because while she had been hiding at Cayelle, people who understood that illegal trade of rift material from Project Charon caused the growth of the pirate fleet held her up as a hero.

Well, fancy that.

She said, "If I was ever brave, I'm rather tired of being brave. Maybe you can all be brave with me."

"I'm sure we will."

Tina gave a command to turn off the light.

"So how was this ship captured, anyway?" she asked in the dark. "Wasn't this supposed to be an invincible war ship?"

"They trapped us," Rae said. "There were too many of them. Hundreds of ships. They knew we were coming because they broke into our communication. They isolated us from the rest of the fleet, because they were familiar with our communication signals."

"And you're saying that someone passed them that information?"

"That definitely happened. I've seen the reports from the bridge."

"Do you know who?"

"Yes, someone who used to be in communication."

"No one currently on board?"

"No, the captain shot him when it came out, point blank, in the brig. Few people are aware that this happened, but they asked me to witness the execution, in my capacity as a medical officer."

Ouch.

"Just to be clear, this captain was not Aliz?" Because the first pilot and captain were not usually the same person.

"No, although she was there, too."

That put some perspective on Aliz's cautious behaviour. She didn't want to talk about it, and she didn't want a repeat.

"It was done in between the time that the ship was surrounded and our commands disabled and that the pirates boarded the ship. The captain said that if they forced us to work for the pirates, he would destroy the ship."

"With all of you on board."

"Yes."

She said nothing for a while, and Tina tried to stop her mind from imagining horrible scenarios.

"But instead, the pirates came on board and they took all of us prisoner, the old-fashioned way."

"Did you see what happened to the other two thousand crew?"

"No. They marched us into the prison in groups. They locked us up where you found us a few days later. We yelled at each other a lot in that building, but increasingly, other groups went quiet."

So the group that contained Vito, Gerry and Stan had indeed only been in treatment for a short period.

They fell quiet, and not much later, Tina could hear Rae's

quiet breathing. She stared into the darkness a bit more, but she was tired and had slept poorly the previous night, and she slept well until voices in the corridor woke her.

They turned out to belong to Lisette and Clodine on their way to breakfast.

Tina quickly went back inside the cabin and got changed. Rae was still asleep. Her hand stuck out of the sleeping bag and twitched occasionally.

Tina caught up with the two women in the passage.

From behind, they couldn't be more different. Clodine was the traditional stick-like somewhat masculine military type, while Lisette was all curves.

They were talking about the noises the ship made at night.

Apparently, the women normally occupied different parts of the ship, and they had to get used to the unfamiliar sounds.

"But I think all those cracks and pops are kind of scary," Lisette was saying. "Where we normally are, the ship doesn't make those sounds. It makes you worry about what Aliz said, that she noticed the ship might have been damaged."

"I think that's the least we have to worry about," Clodine said. "It would be engine damage she's talking about. This ship is sturdy."

"But she said that the engine overheated."

"That would affect the operation of the engine, not the structure of the ship."

Clodine glanced over her shoulder, spotting Tina. She smiled.

"Good morning. It's a good free morning, isn't it? Second free morning already. I could get used to this."

Was there a blunter way to tell Lisette that she was complaining too much?

"Sure," Tina said. She wasn't going to get involved in arguments.

Seriously, were there any people on this ship who didn't

have arguments with each other?

They entered the kitchen where Margot and Gisele were already at work.

To Tina's relief, Finn and Thor were already there, even if Rex and Rasa were not.

Finn informed her he'd slept poorly because he wasn't used to sleeping in Zero-G anymore. Tina thought Thor looked much more tired than Finn, but he didn't complain about it. As usual, Thor listened carefully. He could tell so much from people's voices and other sounds.

Gisele came to the serving area with a tray of covered cups. Clodine lifted one side of the lid and sniffed.

"What's this? It smells great."

"Are these real eggs?" Lisette said.

"Yeah, they are, isn't it great?" Zafira said.

"It's been a long time since I had anything resembling a real egg," said Clodine.

"Didn't you come on a troop carrier? They have chickens," said Miriam. Vito hung on next to her, already eating.

"These are goose eggs," Yonta said.

Margot smiled. "They are indeed, thanks to our visitors. And we have some curry as well. Do you want eggs?" The latter to Tina.

"No, I'll… let you have them."

Damn, she couldn't bring herself to deny the women their treat. She had no proof that eating the eggs was in any way harmful. In fact, it would probably be fine to eat them. But still…

Finn and Thor weren't eating the eggs either. When Margot offered, they had said that they were getting rather sick of them. And that there weren't enough for the women anyway, so they had rather share their portion.

"How did they get the eggs?" Tina asked Finn quietly.

"I don't know. Apparently Rasa mentioned the geese, and

Margot wouldn't let go of the idea that they could have fresh eggs."

Tina watched while the women ate, but didn't see anyone breaking out in feathers, so she forced herself to stop worrying about it. They had so many more pressing things to do.

Then someone called out, "Gerry!"

Everyone turned to the door.

It was Gerry indeed, looking scruffy and dirty, with stubble on his face and scuff marks over his clothes.

He floated into the kitchen and took a holdfast place at the end of the dining bar.

"I figured I should come to say sorry to all of you," he said into the silence. "Seems I made a bit of an idiot of myself. I don't know what was wrong with me, but I just got really angry for no reason, probably from being cooped up in here."

"You've been 'cooped up' for like all of two days. And obviously you didn't serve on the ship when it was at full occupancy," Yonta said.

"We don't mind, do we?" Miriam said, glaring at Yonta, and Yonta ignored her glare.

Yonta very much looked like she did mind.

"Make sure it doesn't happen again," Cally said. "We need everyone to pull their weight."

"I'm OK now," Gerry said. He even sounded demure.

Tina wasn't buying it.

Gerry joined Miriam and Vito at the holdfast bar and took his breakfast from Gisele.

Tina kept looking at him while he ate rather quickly. She could imagine that he was hungry.

Margot came to the serving area with a tray of bowls, which she started handing out to everyone.

Stan lifted a tiny corner of the lid so that he could see what was inside. "Where are the beans?"

"It's curry and fresh eggs. Real ones."

"I want beans," Stan insisted.

"Well, there are none today," Margot said. "It looks like the pirates have taken off with our supply of them. I wish them many smelly meals."

Several women laughed.

"I want beans," Stan said, as if she had said nothing.

"I said there are none."

Stan pushed himself off from the central food bar. He floated through the cabin with disturbing precision towards the storage and cooking areas.

"What are you doing?" Margot said.

"I said I wanted beans. I am going to get the fucking beans."

"Stop it," Yonta said. Her voice was loud enough to cut through the noise Stan made.

"It's my right to have beans. You can't stop me getting beans."

"Vito, tell him to calm down," Miriam said, turning to her partner.

But Vito did nothing, and Miriam got angry as well. "Come on, you're his mate. Stop him being such an idiot."

Vito shrugged. "What? He's grown up and can look after himself."

Meanwhile, Stan had gone inside the storage area and was opening cupboards, pulling out the contents, letting them float in the air.

"Stop making a mess of my kitchen," Margot said.

"You can't stop me getting my beans."

"Oh yes, I can. This is my kitchen, and if I tell you to stop, you—"

"I. Want. My. Beans!"

He shouted like a madman, the whites of his eyes showing and spit flying from his mouth.

Margot and Yonta grabbed him by his clothes. They wrestled him out of the kitchen into the dining area.

There, Clodine helped secure him into a seat.

Vito brought him a food container. Stan ate, no longer asking about beans.

Tina felt chilled inside. If these three men got angry and really wanted to, they could scuttle the whole survival plan and kill all of them.

Getting some food into him made Stan calm down.

He ate his breakfast and drank his juice without saying another word.

Tina then took the two remaining cups of breakfast for Aliz and Evelle on the bridge, making sure that she didn't bring them any eggs. She wasn't going to mention that they had real eggs on board. Aliz was the one person who was truly indispensable in this group. If something happened to her, then they were well and truly screwed.

Aliz and Evelle were both at the controls, talking to each other in detailed and technical jargon. Tina hung back a bit to let them finish whatever they were doing.

She thought Aliz was getting handover notes from Evelle, who was about to go to sleep.

They both took their cups and ate in silence.

"I got some messages from headquarters," Aliz said. "They're not very helpful, but it seems they are aware of our situation, and they will probably try to send someone, even though the message says nothing about it."

Tina knew about this. These types of messages were always full of double meanings, because you never knew who intercepted your communication.

"Do you think anyone will come?" she asked.

"They will, but whether they will come in time is another matter. For us, that is. But they will fight to retain control of this ship, even if we're no longer here."

"Is this ship that important?"

"Hell, it is."

CHAPTER FIFTEEN

TINA RETURNED to the kitchen where all the crew members were still talking to each other. Rex and Rasa had shown up while she had been at the bridge.

Both of them looked much more cheerful than the rest of the crew.

At least someone was having fun.

Aliz had told her she would also come down to the mess to address the crew about what they were going to do today, now that the engineer situation had improved with Finn and Thor on board.

She turned up a bit later, carrying a device with a few blinking lights on her left wrist that she checked occasionally.

Everyone gathered around at the central hold fast bar, waiting for her to speak.

"I did some diagnostic tests on the engines, and it seems that overheating damaged the second auxiliary engine. It needs a service, and some parts replaced."

"I can do that," Finn said.

"And I can help him," Thor said.

Aliz continued, "We need to do this first before we do

anything else. I am not willing to engage the main engine again until we have fixed this. It has the potential to do further damage, and if that happens we would need to go into a station for repairs in dock. There is no station where we can do that safely. I'll speak with Finn and Thor later about what checks we need to run on the main engine. But meanwhile, we are going to give the ship a complete check over. I'm going to divide you up into teams, and I want you to report on every power socket and device in every room. I want all the lights to be checked, and all the computers and any device you encounter. Report in with me when you're in a certain area, and I will tell you where to go and which tests to perform. I will stay at the bridge, and I may get pretty busy, so I need all of you to be patient. This entire process of checking may take more than a day, and may require more than one team. I want all of you to dress in heavy duty maintenance overalls, because I have powered down some areas of the ship, and it may be pretty cold. I want all of you to carry air monitors and breathing apparatus in case that's necessary. I can't guarantee that the air quality is going to be adequate in all parts of the ship. Be careful."

There were nods all around.

Clodine wanted to know, "How did you go with contacting the fleet?"

Aliz's face darkened. "I heard back from some, but mostly they seem to be scattered, and the group of Federacy Force ships we spotted outside the system is under order to stay put. Apparently, a large pirate fleet is due in the system and their function is to stop them."

Several people laughed at this.

"But I am worried that they received specific orders to defend the system against a much larger pirate fleet. I would have expected for them to be ordered to regroup and join up with other groups. In fact, there hasn't really been much in the way of sense coming out of headquarters."

"What else do you expect?" Cally asked.

Yonta snorted. "Yeah, they only think about themselves and their leadership medals."

Aliz continued, "I don't think we can expect a lot of help from headquarters. This makes it official. We have several options. We can fix the engine, which we have to do anyway, then we can join them. They are not very far away, and we would make it there even with half an engine, but I doubt we could give them any assistance, although they may lend us some crew, but that would weaken their ability to respond to this incoming pirate invasion."

"And what would that do to our crew members remaining on Aurora Station?" Yonta asked.

"Yes, I don't want to leave them, and we should go back for them," Miriam said.

She sat next to Gerry and Stan, who had been laughing and whispering to each other. They now glanced at her and fell silent. Gerry scratched his arms. The top of his forearms bore red marks from his nails.

Rae was glaring at them from across the food preparation bar.

"I agree we should go back to the station to rescue the rest of the crew," Margot said. "You talk about capable crew, and those people are the most capable of all, because they already know the ship, and they know us, and they're our mates."

"Yeah," Zafira said.

So they were back to that discussion.

"What are you even talking about?" Thor said.

Tina cringed. She wished she'd taken the time to warn him and Finn about the sensitivity of that subject in this group.

"The rest of the crew of this ship, who got left at the station," Zafira explained.

"Weren't they brought in as prisoners?"

When Thor said something like this, without looking at anyone because he couldn't, it felt doubly eerie.

"They were. We have to free them."

"You can't. Take it from me. We tried."

A shocked silence followed his words.

Thor continued, "We've lost people at the station for years. None of them ever came back. The pirates take them away in their ships. If you look at the station logs, you can see that they usually bring in troop carriers when they close the docks. They bring in prisoners and take away others. They deliberately infect people with rift material. That's what they're doing in those big tubes you've all seen."

"They're just stasis pods," Miriam said. "We saw them, too. We got Vito, Stan and Gerry out. They're all right."

That, of course, was the big question.

Tina doubted the men were anywhere near as "all right" as Miriam claimed, with all the strange behaviour, and now Gerry had been scratching his arms for most of breakfast. And the crew still at the station would have been subjected to the treatment for longer.

But the women obviously didn't want to see that, for as long as they didn't know what Tina knew.

"You seem to think that we can just barge into the station and rescue the remaining crew with a group as small as this," Tina said.

"That's what you did," Lisette said.

"The pirates were unaware that I was at the station and we came from within. I had local help."

"There is no reason we can't do something similar," Miriam said.

No, there wasn't.

But Thor snorted. "This ship wouldn't even be allowed to

dock at the station. It has a Federacy ID tag. The station would block access straight away. Same for the fighters."

"We have your ship," Zafira said.

She met Tina's eyes with her fierce brown gaze.

Tina felt the ground slipping from under her.

No, just no.

The *Alethia* was her entire life, and she was *not* going to risk it for a futile operation like this. This was a bunch of highly compromised people who were at severe risk of being already too far gone.

Just no.

How else could she make her point? Thor had been blunter than she would have been. Thor had told the truth, but these women failed to understand, like they refused to believe what was happening to their mates. And Tina had no proof that presented the data in a way they could understand.

"How about we force the station to allow us to dock?" Stan said.

"How?"

"Easy. We got cannons. They don't. We threaten to shoot them. Then they will give us what we want." The tone in his voice chilled Tina.

"It is not like that," Finn said.

"What do you know about it?"

"I served on big ships."

"So have I. You have no right to tell me I'm dumb."

"I didn't say—"

"Yes, you did."

"I am the engineer you so badly wanted," Finn said, raising his voice. "If you still want my services, I want you to be smart and not to squander the work I'm going to put into fixing your engine."

"I looked you up. You are just a rich boy."

"This 'just a rich boy' is your engineer. Without me, you're not going anywhere."

Stan laughed. "Are you threatening us? We are free citizens. You can't force us to do anything."

"Well then, let us go again. We'll get on with our lives and let you get on with your miserable lives rattling around this ship."

Tina grabbed him by the arm. "Finn, calm down."

She had never seen him like this.

"But these guys are idiots."

Tina spoke to Finn in a soft voice. "I know. I think there is something wrong with him. We rescued them from incubation cubicles in the ship. I haven't told you the story yet, but it's quite horrific. I think that something has affected their minds."

"Are you suggesting we're mad?" Gerry said.

Finn placed himself in front of Tina. "Threaten her, mate, and you'll deal with me."

"Finn, Gerry, please."

Both men fell quiet.

Tina pulled Finn back.

Finn and Stan looked at each other, eyeing each other and waiting for the other party to start arguing again.

But they retreated and made a show of not looking at each other.

Gerry was still scratching his arms.

Rex and Rasa watched next to each other, wide-eyed. Jens, too, looked on.

Tina was overcome with a sense of dread.

What had she brought her friends into?

The bad thing was that they couldn't leave again, because it required cooperation from a lot of other people, and she didn't want to leave the women stranded with nowhere to go. And she didn't want to leave Evelle with them either. And Evelle would never leave the ship.

"Let's solve our problems one by one," she said, after having schooled her voice into more neutral tones. She turned to Aliz.

Aliz divided people into groups, with each group containing one technologically experienced and one lesser technologically experienced person. Each team was going to get an earpiece and testing equipment.

Tina paired up with Rex, although he would have greater knowledge of technology than some of the crew, especially the ones who worked in administration or the kitchens.

Rasa chose to stay on board the *Alethia*. She said she had to feed the geese, but Tina suspected she was also highly suspicious of the military crew.

Finn and Thor would go together, and Clodine and Lisette, who seem to be friendly with each other, and Yonta and Cally, and so on.

"What about us?" Gerry asked.

"You can go with Miriam," Aliz said.

"I want to go with someone to do important jobs," Gerry said.

Stan said, "Yes, I don't understand why they get all the interesting jobs."

"There is nothing terribly interesting about any of these jobs," Aliz said. "If you can help, you can go together."

Gerry said, "I want to get one of those earpieces, too."

Stan agreed. "Yes, you're giving special favours to them. Because we're men and they're women."

But Aliz deflected the barb masterfully. "I thought, being strong men and all, you might do some other jobs for me that women are not so good at."

But Tina sensed that Aliz also didn't trust the men, especially in line with what happened with the airlock.

"I don't want to be treated any different," Stan said.

Vito said, "He's right. You're all against us."

"We are making use of the unique abilities of each of the crew members," Rae said.

She spoke so little in conversations that people took notice when she did.

"We rescued you, and we're sparing you because you may still be recovering. If you want to work, that's fine, but I'm the doctor and I will need to clear you for active duty."

"I thought we weren't doing rules anymore," Gerry said.

"This is a rule I will adhere to for as long as I'm aboard this ship. I can't have people working when they're not up to it and then blaming the Force when something goes wrong."

CHAPTER SIXTEEN

TINA RETURNED to her cabin to get changed into her overalls. While she was getting them out of her bag, the door opened again and Rae came in.

"I was hoping you'd be here. I'd like to speak to you in person," she said.

"Is there a problem?" Tina asked.

Rae went to the cabin door and made sure it was shut. Then she faced Tina, her expression serious.

"I think I found out who is passing on information to the pirates," she said.

"Oh? Did something happen since you last mentioned it?"

Which was only yesterday. It was incredible how long ago that seemed.

"This morning, I had to go to the administration section to look something up on the medical system. Lisette was still sitting at the computer. She seemed nervous when I said hello."

"Couldn't she just be doing communication? I had some interaction with her yesterday, when she offered to send my material to Olympus for me."

And Tina hadn't gone ahead with it, because she had been wondering about the trustworthiness of the people who would receive it.

"There is no reason for her to be there," Rae said. "We're a small group of people in a giant ship that's going nowhere without orders. It's not like we can resume our normal operations. Also, the fact that the ship fell into enemy hands means that we can't access the Force's database any more until we've been vetted and found safe. She couldn't have been communicating with the command in a regular way. Only Aliz can do that."

"Maybe she was trying to contact her family," Tina said.

"Maybe, but do keep an eye on her, because she seemed nervous."

Tina wondered if being paranoid was part of Rae's normal state of mind, and whether or she needed to give this remark any weight without further evidence. Like Finn, Rae came from that world of the rich families of Olympus, and those people seemed to have a permanent state of suspicion engraved on their soul.

"There is actually something I was wondering about," Tina said.

"Oh, any other suspicious behaviour?"

"No, but I was wondering if you did the medical checkup for the three men we rescued."

"I did a cursory checkup. They seemed a bit shaken, but otherwise fine. Why?"

"Didn't you notice how Gerry was constantly scratching himself at breakfast?"

"There were a lot of strange things about Gerry this morning. The air inside the ships makes people's skin dry. Skin irritation is very common after stasis."

"I think it could also mean something else. Is there a way for you to ask the men to come in for another checkup?"

"I would need a good reason. They were all pretty reluctant, especially Gerry. Even before we were captured, he was always reluctant to come. He says he doesn't like doctors, and I suspect he doesn't like female doctors in particular."

"Any reason?"

"He never trusted me enough to tell me. He would make appointments and then make excuses not to attend them. Some people are like that, for as long as they're healthy, it's not worth the fight to make them turn up. If I suspect that there is something going on with his health, I can go to his supervisor to make him come to a medical examination, but I've never had reason to do so."

"I would like you to find an excuse to do it."

"Well... That's not going to be easy in the current climate. He has lost his immediate supervisor. I doubt he'd listen to Yonta. He might listen to Aliz, but she has other things on her mind. Do you have a reason to want it?"

"The mutation that turns people into the warty toads that we call 'pirates' starts with a skin condition. I'll give you the short version of what I know."

Judging by the sound of talk, people in the hallway were getting ready for their tasks of checking parts of the ship that Aliz had assigned to them. So, as quickly as she could, she told Rae about the infection and what she had discovered. From the pirates and strange creature at Gandama, Simon Fosnet and the little girl Molly, to the cactuses and her work at Project Charon, and what she had seen in the far end of the large laboratory rooms where they had rescued Gerry, Vito and Stan.

During the talk, Rae's eyes widened.

"You mean these people are actively turning prisoners into mutants?"

"Mutant soldiers. Replicas of themselves. They're diminished as human beings. Once people have gone through this process, they are appear to be stronger, and there have been rumours that they also live longer, but that is if they get through the transformation process without dying, and not everyone does."

"So you think that the three men might be on this path?"

"I don't know. We rescued them from the process. I have no idea what treatment they already received. That is why I haven't said anything about it. We have to keep a very close eye on them."

Rae looked disturbed.

"I guess I could ask them to come in for another checkup."

"Do that. Please."

She let out a breath. "Do the women know any of this?"

"I don't think so. They've seen their crew mates in the cubicles, but they don't know why the men were there and what happens to people during the process."

"How long does a person need to stay in before the change is irreversible?"

Tina shrugged. "Your guess is as good as mine."

"Is that what they want then? Turn us all into pirates?"

"I don't think we can rule out anything. I've met the pirate leader and it wouldn't surprise me if he wants to create vast armies of followers. Those people, once they're too far gone, aren't people anymore and you can't argue with them. But even before that time, something changes about the way they react to other people. They become aggressive, callous. Even if the process is long, and the three men have been infected but can recover, we'll need to restrict their contact with the rest of us. I need your help to achieve that."

"The women won't like that. We need the men to help. They don't exhibit any symptoms. You can't convince the women that their mates are compromised when they act normally."

"Creating silly arguments over beans, or opening air lock doors is behaving normally?"

Rae's eyes widened.

"By the time they show more serious symptoms, it will be too late."

CHAPTER SEVENTEEN

TINA MET Rex in the corridor outside her room.

"Oh, there you are," he said. "I was wondering if you'd started without me."

"My roommate wanted to have a talk."

"Something important?"

"Not for what we're doing today. She is a doctor. You should make an appointment to see her."

Rex pulled a face.

Tina grinned. She knew Rex was very much over having to visit doctors. She wanted his attachment points checked out just in case, but Rex's new harness made these visits much less important.

Behind her, Rae was also leaving the cabin, dressed in her service overalls. Gisele, who was to be Rae's team mate, waited in the corridor.

Aliz had told the teams to go to the supplies depot, where Clodine would give each team a set of measuring tools.

Aliz had come down from the bridge, but said she'd soon go back because apparently there was a fair bit of communication going on in the area.

"Are they reopening the station?" Margot asked, her voice hopeful.

"It doesn't involve the station. We're picking up messages from the Freeranger ships in multiple languages. I want to listen in to see if I can figure out what they're talking about."

"Finn might help with that," Tina said.

"Yeah, he told me. I think he has better things to do. I'll record anything I can intercept."

She returned to the bridge, while Tina and Rex and the other teams dispersed over the ship.

Aliz had explained that while she had full control of the ship from the bridge, nothing replaced a full manual assessment.

She needed to know which check points still gave the correct testing responses. Tina understood about those and only needed to have a quick look at the program before she understood how to work it. The *Alethia* had similar diagnostic software. Only simpler. Much simpler.

By running the software at each of these points, Aliz would get a picture of the damage to the ship, its computer systems and power supply.

All this while Finn and Thor—with Jens to carry their tools—descended into the engine housing to assess the damage there.

Aliz would then feed all that information into her diagnostics, and it would tell her the health and current capabilities of the ship.

A ship like this was a hugely complex network of the most advanced technology. Being properly trained, Aliz would have a responsibility not to endanger the ship or its crew.

Tina and Rex made a quick way down the corridor to their allocated section, which was in the central part of the ship in between the kitchens and the power plant that operated the shields and weapons.

True to Aliz's word, the lights were all on and crisp filtered air hissed out of the vents. A little too crisp at times.

For a long time, the work was pretty boring. They moved from room to room.

Rex used his metal fingers to lever panels off the walls, and then Tina connected the diagnostics tools.

It was very quiet. They didn't see any other people.

As far as Tina could see, the results all came back good.

Meanwhile, Rex was talking with Jens and kept telling Tina about what Finn and Thor found in the engines.

Apparently, Finn reported some overheating damage, and he was getting Jens to collect engine parts from the supply store with a special trolley that, according to Jens, was really cool, like a mini-spaceship.

"It flies through the corridors," Rex said. "If we wait at this intersection here, he says he's going to come past so we can see it."

"We are supposed to be working."

"But I want to see this," Rex said.

Tina supposed she should start on the data entry and mark off on the map which areas they had tested.

So they waited in the corridor, but Jens took his time, and when Tina had caught up with her data entry, there was still no sign of him.

"Come on, I finished entering all our data. I think we should continue."

"I've asked him where he is, but he's not responding," Rex said.

"I'm guessing they're doing their work, like we should be."

"Jens always responds to me."

"That's when he's not working for someone else," Tina said.

But eventually, Rex gave in. He gave a last look down the passage, but there was no sign of Jens and his trolley.

They turned back into the side passage and continued with their work.

Then a voice drifted down the corridor. "Rex, Rex."

"That is Jens," Rex said, and he pushed himself back towards the main passage.

It was indeed Jens, but he was not with his cool vehicle.

He pulled himself along the walls with incredible speed and almost crashed into Rex. His face was pale and his eyes wide.

"What happened?" Rex asked.

"The guy just went crazy," Jens said, panting. His face was sweaty.

"Which guy?"

Tina had a very bad feeling about this.

"I don't remember his name. The one with the moustache. He came out of a room and kicked me off. He said those trolleys were his, and we weren't supposed to use them, and then he took off with it."

"Did he hurt you?" Tina asked. That sounded like Vito.

"He pushed me into the wall. It didn't hurt, but he took off with all the things I was taking to Dad."

"Did he say what he was going to do with it?"

These were likely to be important parts for the engine, and the ship stores had very limited supplies of those.

"No, but if he wanted my job, he could have just asked and we could have done it together."

"Was he alone?"

"No, the woman who sat next to him this morning was with him. She was in the door to a room, yelling at him."

Tina needed to report this to Aliz immediately. She activated her earpiece.

"Aliz, I think we have a problem. I think Vito has become upset. He has taken Jens' trolley and is loose in the ship."

"I have already located him," Aliz said. "He harassed Thor

and said that he was going to take over his job, because apparently he has suddenly developed into an engineer."

"What happened?" Tina couldn't imagine that Finn would allow anyone to disturb his work.

"Apparently, there was a minor altercation. Finn reports that he got the parts."

"Finn is all right?"

"I haven't heard, but assume so. I told him to abandon the task immediately and return to the mess. I want you to do the same. Our people are more important than the job. We can always do the job later. We need to make sure that everyone can work safely."

Tina and Rex returned to the mess, where she found several people already gathered. Margot had returned to the kitchen earlier to make lunch, but none of the men were there. Neither was Miriam.

Everyone wanted to know what was going on, and Rex's stories understandably disturbed people.

"I am sure this is just a misunderstanding," Sarina said.

"Misunderstanding, my arse," Yonta said. "Gerry takes command of the docking hall while I'm away, Stan gets into an argument about beans, for fuck's sake, and Vito tries to disrupt the delivery of engine parts. They're trying to sabotage us, that's what."

"But why would they do that? Their survival depends on our survival, too."

"Don't expect me to explain the logic of men."

Yes, Tina had heard about Yonta's preference for women in all aspects of her life.

Finn, Thor and Jens had also not yet returned. When Tina asked about it, Aliz said that once Finn had taken apart certain engine parts, he would have to finish the job.

Tina didn't like this one bit. "I'll go down to help them."

She felt guilty about drawing Finn and Thor into this. They

had expected to be on their way to Olympus, not to be drawn into this death trap of a ship.

She quickly made her way through the passages and had some trouble finding the right entry point to the engine chamber. The ship's engine compartment was huge, much larger than she had expected.

She found Finn and Thor at work in a control station, where they had pulled an entire section of panels out of the wall. The power was off, and both Finn and Thor carried lights, although Thor's light beamed sideways at Finn's hands. Finn was calling out instructions.

Jens was also in the room, floating at a lower level with a bunch of leads which he plugged into a panel when Finn told him to.

It was Thor who said, "Someone's here."

All three turned to the entrance. The wide-eyed looks on their faces showed how tense they were.

"Aliz wants you all back in the mess where she knows everyone is safe. Vito is still on the loose."

"I can't leave all the engine's electronics open," Finn said.

"Then close it up as quickly as you can."

"I'll need the captain's guarantee that the engine won't be engaged."

He asked for, and got, the guarantee.

Tina could hear Aliz's tinny voice through the loudspeaker. "I want you secure. Once we've resolved the situation, you can finish it in the next couple of days."

"We need a lot more than a few days," Thor said under his breath.

Yes, Tina spotted sections of burnt out electronics on the panel that would need to be replaced for the engine to have full operation. Whatever optimistic view Aliz presented, talking about "some damage" and that "checks were needed before engaging the main engine", it was painfully clear that the ship was nowhere near healthy. They would have to face the reality that they would need to return to the station to have it fixed, if there was anyone at the station capable of performing that task.

They returned to the mess not much later, where most other people had also turned up, including Evelle, who looked sleepy and cranky, but who had been to the stores and had collected an assortment of nondestructive weaponry and handed out stunners and extendable batons to whoever wanted one.

While Tina had been away, Aliz had explained that they might need to restrict whoever didn't behave themselves, and that they might need to isolate those people from the rest of the crew.

They agreed that the small hospital was probably the best place for that, because it had an isolation ward.

"Just to observe them, mind," Rae said. "I'll tell them they have chemicals in their blood that make them angry, and we don't want anyone to get hurt until their blood is normal."

"Yeah, I didn't like the way Stan argued about his breakfast," Gisele said. "Like he would have attacked me if I didn't give him beans. Lucky all you guys were here."

Several women nodded.

Even Yonta found nothing snarky to say.

Tina and Rex helped Rae prepare the room by taking out anything that was not bolted to the floor or walls.

No one said much while they were doing this. A sense of dread hung over everyone.

Rex put a metal hand on Tina's shoulder.

"Hey, those guys won't do anything to me. I can rip them to pieces."

"Thank you. I'd rather you didn't do that. It's messy."

It was a joke, but there was no guarantee that this horrible thing wouldn't come to pass. Tina had no reason to disbelieve that Rex could really do this. She did question how his young mind would cope if it happened.

Tina realised that she had left behind one of the diagnostics tools when they had met Jens. It wasn't far, so she went to pick it up. Rex insisted on coming.

"I didn't like that none of those guys had turned up when Aliz asked them to come," he said.

No, Tina didn't like it either, but she didn't want to plant any more worry in his mind. "They've been like that since the beginning. They don't say a lot and don't always react to what people tell them. They're still recovering."

But as she said that, someone screamed down the corridor.

CHAPTER EIGHTEEN

TINA PUSHED herself out of the room, into the corridor.

She called out, "Where are you? Do you need help?"

The passage was deserted, with no indication of where the sound had come from. Her voice echoed in the emptiness.

From that pressing, stifling silence came a soft groan, the direction impossible to tell.

A loud clang made the floor vibrate. It came from further down the corridor, as if a door fell shut. Someone fleeing?

The groan came again. Definitely a voice, a *female* voice.

Tina pushed herself in that direction, followed by Rex.

She looked into room after room, but couldn't see anything out of the ordinary in any of the storerooms on either side.

Then Rex called out, "Mum, come over here."

He had been behind her, so she turned around, but the corridor behind her was empty.

"Where are you?" Her heart jumped.

"Over here, in the small parts storeroom."

Tina entered the room—there was a sign next to the door—and finally found him behind a storage unit.

With him was a woman in ship overalls. She floated in the

air, her hair loose and wet on one side. A rip in one of her sleeves showed the suit liner underneath.

"Oh no, Miriam."

She was half conscious, hanging in the air behind him as if caught in a picture, her head butting softly into the side of the storage unit.

Globules of blood floated around her, jiggling and changing shape in the way fluid did in weightlessness. Miriam had a deep gash in her shoulder where a sharp object had gone through her overalls. Blood was seeping out, the source of the globules in the surrounding air.

Tina turned around to the entrance where, as in all military ships she had travelled on, she found the first aid cabinet.

She yanked open the door, grabbed a couple of rolls of bandages and returned to Miriam.

"Miriam, Miriam, can you hear me?"

Her lips moved, but her voice was a mere mumble, too soft for Tina to understand.

"Hang in there, I will help you. Call Rae." The latter to Rex. He disappeared into the corridor.

Tina ripped Miriam's overalls down with the aid of the pathetic little scissors that seemed to be part of every first aid kit. She exposed the wound. Blood welled up from a sharp cut in Miriam's shoulder. It didn't look terribly deep. She could see no other injuries.

"Did you hit your head?"

"I don't know. It hurts." Her voice was a mere whisper.

"Who did this?"

"He's out there somewhere," she whispered.

"Who? Vito?"

Because the two had been in a team together and neither had turned up when Aliz called the crew to the mess.

"I wouldn't come with him."

"Come with him, where? Was it Vito?"

"He wanted to take the ship... go to the station to rescue the others... I said we would do that, but he wanted them to join his gang... the pirates. He said... what's the leader's name?"

"Artan?"

"Yes... that one... he would reward all of us."

"What did you say? Did you agree?" Rae's suggestion that there was a mole on board would not leave her alone.

Miriam shook her head. "They scare me... you know how they treated us. They locked us up and would walk past the door and would make terrible comments. But I thought that Vito..."

A tear ran over her cheek and floated into the air.

"We can talk later. Rae should be here soon so she can treat your shoulder."

"It burns."

"Yes, you received a nasty cut."

"No, it burns all over. It seeps through my arm. Like crawling ants. It hurts." Her expression was distant and eyes unfocused.

"Don't worry. We will help you."

She looked around. Rex was still in the corridor, talking to someone. She could hear his voice.

She wondered where Vito was and guessed it had been him slamming the door earlier.

She bandaged up Miriam's shoulder to stop the bleeding. Miriam complained about the pain. Her speech grew more incoherent and slurred.

Tina didn't like it.

Rae came in, took one look and went straight to the victim. She also examined Miriam, commented on the bandaging. It was a little too tight for her liking. She also did not find a sign of other injuries.

Miriam had lost consciousness, and Rae had to put her

head in a bracket to stop it lolling and potentially hitting something.

"It worries me," she told Tina as they were transporting Miriam back to the hospital.

They installed Miriam in the onboard hospital, which was well-equipped and efficient.

Rae attached Miriam to some monitors.

"Do you want me to help?" Tina asked.

"Bring me some food," Rae said.

"Sure, I can do that."

Tina made her way to the kitchen where she found everyone else already gathered.

Margot had produced a meal, but no one was complaining about the lack of variety, or, for that matter, the lack of beans.

Stan and Gerry were also in the room, and Tina had an insane desire to send them out. She already suspected Gerry, and Stan hadn't yet done anything unusual, but she suspected him, too.

Aliz had obtained the security footage from the room where they had found Miriam.

It showed Vito and Miriam in an argument, then they appeared to make up and embraced, at which point Vito produced a knife and cut her shoulder.

Miriam fought him, and then he pushed her away and fled the room.

"Why the hell did he do that?" Zafira called out.

"Wait, play that again. It makes no sense to me," Cally said.

Aliz replayed the recording, which everyone watched in silence.

Tina glanced at Rex and Jens. The recording was in colour and clearly showed blood spraying out of the wound. She didn't like it that Rex and Jens saw this.

"What the hell did he think he was doing?" Sarina said.

"I never trusted that creep," Yonta said.

But Tina noticed something as Vito pushed his struggling girlfriend away and made for the door.

He seemed to push his hand deliberately into the open wound. And why was the back of his shirt pink?

Everyone agreed they needed to restrict Vito's movements, and they discussed how to do that. Tina didn't like that the other two men were still in the room.

She collected two portions of dinner—one for Rae and one for Miriam just in case she felt like eating—and left again.

CHAPTER NINETEEN

TINA MADE the trip to the hospital, where Rae was still looking after Miriam. It didn't look like Miriam was going to be interested in eating soon, but Tina left both containers in the hospital anyway, even if Rae would eat both.

Rae said she would stay in the hospital. She didn't make any comments on Miriam's state.

Tina told Rae to make sure that the main entrance to the hospital was locked, in case Vito wanted to create trouble.

"If they're partners, he's legally able to see her if he wants to press the matter," Rae said.

"Don't let him in. Make some sort of excuse. But just lock the door. Please."

Rae said that she would need to get the approval from the Captain to do that, but that, failing the Captain, Aliz would have to do.

Even when faced with an obvious threat, she still thought of future implications of her actions.

She was cautious and suspicious. It must be awful to grow up thinking that every person out there was likely to drag you before the court because they thought you had money.

Tina returned to the mess hall to get supplies for Aliz and Evelle on the bridge. She met the rest of the women who were going the other way, led by Clodine. They were on their way to the supplies stores to collect gear to protect themselves. Tina fished Rex and Jens out of the group.

Neither of the boys had been to the bridge before. They both looked on in wonder.

Evelle was asleep and Aliz sat alone at the controls, the only person in that large room that should be a hive of activity.

"Wow," Jens said, looking around.

Tina thought that without the activity and associated people, the room looked sad.

Tina gave the food container to Aliz, after having put Evelle's portion in the storage compartment.

"Come over here, I wanted to ask you something," Aliz said.

She looked tired, worried and worn out.

They were going to have to do something soon, because they couldn't keep going like this, rattling around in the giant ship with far less crew than necessary to operate it.

"Is there something else I can do for you?" Tina asked, while settling in the second pilot station.

"Yes. I've closed internal access to the docks. Literally every means we have to help ourselves and get this ship back into operation is in that hall and adjacent workshops. I don't want anyone to wander around in there if they shouldn't be. You might want to warn your young girl that she can't get out the usual way."

"I can do that." Tina very much doubted that Rasa *wanted* to get out.

"Also..." Aliz hesitated. "I may seem paranoid to you, but some of these men think they can fly fighters because they have used the simulators. I want you to go to the flight bay and lock all the fighters up. They're normally unlocked, but I'll give you the key. I don't want to run the risk that someone uses any of those craft."

"What about the ones that we moved outside to get the *Alethia* in?"

"They should already be locked. Those docking points have pretty good locking mechanisms. I will give you the codes and equipment to make sure that no one except authorised people can move the fighters. Then I want you to power down the control stations in the docking area so that no one who is not supposed to be in there can create trouble."

"What about my ship and Rasa? She has some animals on board that need to be fed." Just the thought of the mutant geese getting loose in the ship gave her the shivers. And that was if she could entice Rasa to leave the *Alethia*.

"There is a way. I'll show you that, too. Let me take all your metrics."

She scanned Tina's fingerprints and set up authorisation for her to open and close the security locks. Tina insisted for Rex and Jens to come with her because she didn't want to lose sight of them.

Rex could also be authorised because apparently his harness contained a secret code.

"I'm still learning about this thing every day," Rex said. By the look of things, he was enjoying it, too.

When everything was set up, Aliz showed Tina, Rex and Jens the secret: there was an access tunnel that led directly from the bridge to the entry hall. Aliz said that it bypassed all the corridors and sector doors that would shut in emergencies.

"That's handy," Tina said.

"It's so that rescuers will always have a quick entry to the bridge and the pilots have a quick way out. It costs a lot of effort and time to train pilots, and if you gain access to the ship from outside in an emergency, you want to have a quick way to get to the control room."

The tunnel was narrow, only wide enough for one person to pass, especially someone as big as Rex in his harness.

Aliz had turned on the light, but the small emergency lights were blotted out when someone passed close by.

It didn't take them long to reach the docking hall.

The area was deathly quiet. Tina had told Rasa to keep everything shut, and the *Alethia* looked abandoned.

Every little sound they made echoed in the emptiness.

The bay contained another six fighters. Tina extracted her locking device and approached the first one.

"Whoa," Jens said. He was looking into the cabin of the craft through the canopy. "This is exactly like in the simulation."

"Yes, this is why Aliz is afraid that the men will take these craft out. The games make everyone think they can fly this craft. But there is a lot more involved than attacking other ships in open space. The hardest part is getting in and out of your hosting ship. You need experience for that."

"Like you freed us from Kelso Station?" Rex said. He grinned.

"You want to be smart?"

Tina opened the cover, slid into the pilot seat and activated it and Aliz's locking key. The controls that were activated by her presence went dark.

Then she moved to the next craft.

They were at the fourth one when a soft sound came from elsewhere in the hall.

"Did you guys hear that?" she asked.

"Yes."

"Was that Rasa?" She glanced at the dark form of the *Alethia*. They'd noticed no sign that Rasa knew they were here.

"No, it came from over there," Jens said, pointing to the far end of the hall which held tool cabinets of a maintenance station. "I can have a look if you want."

"No, I would prefer that you stay here," Tina said, but Jens had already gone.

"I'll go with him," Rex said.

Tina wasn't happy about this, but she had only two more craft to go, and the job should be done quickly.

She went to the fifth craft and quickly activated the mechanism and then was about to go to the sixth one, but a strangled noise drifted from elsewhere in the hall.

She slammed shut the cover and drifted in the direction that the noise had come from.

"Rex, Jens, where are you?"

Her heart was thudding.

The only reply was further unidentified sounds: a grunt, a crack or slap, something slamming against a metal surface with a *boing*.

"What's going on, Rex?" she called out.

Someone laughed, a dark voice that didn't belong to either Rex or Jens.

Tina took cover behind a pillar.

Rex and Jens floated through the open hall, in the company of another man.

Vito. The skin on his arms was red and lumpy, with oozing sores. He held one arm around Jens' neck and held a weapon pointed at Rex. He was definitely infected.

Tina had some training in Zero-G combat, but she had no doubt that Vito would be much better at it.

She watched in horror as he floated towards the last fighter that he she hadn't been able to disable yet.

Vito laughed.

"You can do whatever you want, but I'm not affected by any of your beautiful stun weapons. You can't stop me."

"Please, he is taking us to the station," Jens called out.

"No, he is not."

Tina pulled out her PCD and called up Aliz. *Found him. Request immediate assistance.*

Vito laughed again.

"Please, he'll kill us," Jens called. His voice was a squeak.

Vito opened the cover of the fighter.

"You can't get out," Tina yelled to him. "The door is shut, and Aliz is not going to open it."

"I don't need your bitch pilot. I'll blow a hole in the door."

Tina sent to Aliz, *Turn off power in the docking hall.*

Aliz had not yet replied to the first message.

Vito first pushed Jens into the craft and secured him in the back, then he tried to do the same with Rex. But Rex was not an easy prey. He swung around and hit Vito on his arm. The blow that should really have made other people scream did nothing to make him release his grip. He was strong and smart, keeping a hold on to both the craft and Rex, by holding onto the back of his belt.

If there was one disadvantage of Rex's armour, it was that the mechanism required space to operate and while the harness could jump, somersault and climb, it wasn't very good at getting into narrow spaces. He tried to twist around, but couldn't reach where Vito held him.

Panic clamped a hand around Tina's heart.

He was going to take both boys, destroy the ship and get away with it. Then he would try to turn both of them into warty toads. The process might kill them, especially Rex.

Tina broke her cover to find something to use as a weapon. She cursed herself for not having taken the Fireseed. It was still on board the *Alethia*.

She yanked oped a cupboard and found a Zero-G vacuum cleaner, the most pathetic weapon of all, but there was nothing for it. She charged forward and beat Vito over the head with the tube.

The impact hurt her wrists, but didn't affect him, and he

pushed her away, sailing through the open space.

Tina yelled into her earpiece. "Anyone who can hear me, send some back up, please."

She received no reply.

She would really have to do this by herself.

She yanked open one of the maintenance cabinets, found a crowbar, and prepared for one more strike, but the moment she was about to push off, a loud clang echoed from elsewhere in the hall. Vito turned his head. A sizzling beam zapped across the space. It hit Vito in the chest and crackled over him.

Holy crap. Someone was using live ammunition.

Tina turned around, but saw nothing. It had sounded suspiciously like the discharge from her own Fireseed. And that could only have come from the *Alethia*, and Rasa.

The crackles were still going over Vito. He opened his mouth as if to scream, frozen in time.

He had let go of Rex, who had freed Jens. They both joined Tina.

Vito gave a roar. He had let go of the fighter and drifted helplessly into the middle of the hall. He tried to get his overalls off, but ended up ripping one sleeve off. His hand tangled in the loose fabric.

He screamed and twisted, but in worming around to get out of his overalls, he only drifted further into the open space. His tether had become detached. It trailed him through the air. Globs of pink stuff separated from his skin, forming into foamy globules. What was that?

At that point, the safety door to the rest of the ship opened, the one that Aliz had closed. Clodine, Cally and Yonta floated through.

Yonta exclaimed, "Shit."

Clodine threw her tether's magnet to the wall where it attached with a clang. The other two grabbed hold of the cable and the three of them kind of hung there, staring at Vito.

"What the hell is all this about?" Yonta said.

"He took a hit," Tina said, looking at Rasa who still hung onto the doorframe of the *Alethia*, her face disturbed. "Don't touch him."

"I had no intention of doing that," Yonta said.

But somehow they needed to stop Vito spreading this pink stuff all over the hall. It might be infectious.

Tina pushed herself to the *Alethia*.

Rasa held her hand over her mouth. She met Tina's eyes with a shocked expression. "Did I kill him?"

"I don't know." She gently tugged at the weapon in Rasa's hands.

"You better give that to me, missy."

Better not have it accidentally go off.

Rasa let go of the gun. Tina turned it off and stuck it in her belt.

"It was very dangerous to use a live weapon inside the ship," she said.

"I know, but it was either that or lose you. I figured there wasn't much risk as long as he was a clear shot. He was going to kill Rex and Jens."

"He said he was going to take us to the station," Jens said. He still looked pale.

"You saved us," Rex said.

Tina asked, "Where did you learn to shoot like that?"

"I said my brother was in the military. He taught me."

Tina wasn't buying it. In the first place, military personnel would never be allowed to take their weapons home and let their family members play with them, and in the second place, they were always stationed away from the civilian bases.

One day, she would have to get to the bottom of this.

She entered the *Alethia*'s storeroom, ignored the racket made by the geese—and stopped there.

CHAPTER TWENTY

THE AIR in the storeroom was full of pink globules the size of the nail on her pinky, some of them clumping together, bumping into the wall, sticking to the ceiling vents and the outside of the plastic containers on the shelves. They floated everywhere except in the cage with the geese, which had probably eaten any of them that came close enough. They were also still attached to the cactus fronds. More of the damn things floated loose all the time.

These were the things Tina had assumed to be fruit when she saw the cactuses yesterday. But they weren't. They were foamy, without a skin or other structure. They were bubbles of foam, formed into globules in weightlessness.

Was this the same pink stuff that Vito was spreading? Without further analysis, she would say yes.

She slammed the door shut, cutting out the honking of the geese.

"What's happening?" Rasa called out behind her. "What's all this pink sticky stuff?"

"Don't touch it!"

"Whoa. I wasn't touching it."

Tina faced her. "You don't give *anyone* any more eggs, understand?"

Rasa's eyes were wide. "But they will spoil. That's wasteful."

"I don't care. Don't eat them. I don't even understand why you gave them to Margot when you *knew* that there is something strange going on with those animals."

This was the sort of stuff that used to infuriate her at Project Charon: people doing dumb things that they *knew* were stupid, but they thought they could get away with or thought "it would be all right."

No, when dealing with infection, things were *never* all right. Seriously.

Tina rummaged through the other storage compartments and eventually found a lasso net engineers used to capture wayward tools if something floated away during EVA. The net was a bit thin for her liking, since its targets were hammers and screwdrivers, not humans. But it would have to do.

When Tina came out of the ship, the others had Vito surrounded while he floated helplessly in the middle of the hall, flailing his arms and trying to grab at anything that came close. Those things included the sticks the women used to push him away when he threatened to float too close to something he could grab.

Capturing him was going to be tricky.

Tina aimed with the harpoon and deployed the net. He saw it coming and tried to deflect it, but he got his fingers caught in the holes, and the rest of the net neatly enclosed him. But the net wasn't very sturdy, and he would soon rip it apart. Cally found a roll of tape and wound it around him.

During all this, he screamed obscenities at the women, until they could get the tape over his mouth.

"Now shut up, or I'll put it over your nose as well," Cally said.

That seemed to do the trick.

When Tina reported to Aliz what had happened and asked what to do now, Aliz said she didn't want him anywhere near the docks, so they pulled the screaming, wriggling parcel into a storeroom behind the maintenance area outside the sector enclosed by the security door to the docks. They made sure there was nothing inside the room that could be turned into a weapon or would allow him to escape. Cally and Yonta tied his tether to a storage rack so that he sat snugly against the metal frame and his arms were jammed in between the rack and his body and didn't have any freedom.

He growled and moaned, his eyes rolling, sweat on his forehead. He was still shedding globules of pink fluid, most of which stuck to the tape.

His breaths came in quick succession.

This was not a healthy man. Tina would have to ask Rae to have a look at him.

But for now, the women left the room and shut the door.

Phew.

They all looked at each other, a circle of harrowed faces, pale and glistening with sweat.

They didn't need to say anything to express worry about the implications. Were the other two men going to behave like this? There might be signs that Gerry was already on that path. And Stan, with his stupid argument about beans.

Yonta jerked her head at the end of the passage.

"We'll have to clean that up."

A trail of pink globules floated in the hallway where they had passed with Vito.

"Whatever you do, don't touch that stuff with your bare hands," Tina said.

"What is it?" Zafira asked.

"I'm not sure, but nothing good."

"Use the vacuum," Yonta said.

Tina remembered Arkady had mentioned a process called

bloom, and that it was a way that the infection could spread to others.

If nothing else, this proved the cactuses suffered the same condition.

She should isolate them.

She hated the thought to destroy them, because they might need them, but she should seal the plants in a room with the geese and not let anyone in without protection.

They returned to the docking hall, where Aliz shut the security compartment door once Tina confirmed everyone was inside, and Tina showed the women the secret passage to the bridge.

When they arrived there, Finn and Thor had returned.

They hung at the communicator and navigator stations, talking to Evelle, who should be asleep, and Aliz who sat in the command chair.

The sorry bunch of exhausted crew also included the two remaining men. Tina didn't trust the men, but as yet, they had done nothing to justify being locked up. In fact, both had made themselves quite useful.

Tina reported on what had happened in the docks, and then Finn and Thor had an even more depressing report about the engine.

"We don't have the crew to fix this," Finn said. "I could do it, but only dockside, and with the help of a couple of accredited maintenance staff, or a suitably programmed robot. I'd need parts as well, although Aliz has told me there may be a chance they're held on board in the store room. We lack someone with knowledge of the storage system to locate the parts. There has been damage to the main engine, and we can't open the reactor shell until it's been properly powered down and decontaminated. I would very much advise against taking the ship anywhere for a long distance. Neither us nor the ship would survive that."

"What about at half speed?" Zafira asked.

"We can't enter a jump at half speed," Clodine said.

A deep silence followed her words.

"So the translation is: we're screwed," Margot said.

"If that's our only option, yes," Aliz said.

"Are there any other options?" Yonta asked.

Another silence.

"You're supposed to be our leader," Yonta said to Tina.

And *now* she acknowledged that? Now that *she* was out of ideas?

Tina resisted a cutting remark, because it wouldn't solve anything.

"We've been fairly... busy in the last twenty-four hours," Tina said. "We need to look at our options."

"Easy. We need to return to the station," Clodine said.

"Easy," Tina repeated. "Return to pick up our crew and it will all be fine."

Several women made agreeing noises before they realised Tina meant it sarcastically. Some glanced at Gerry, who was looking at something on his PCD. Signs that at least he was starting to understand their predicament? Who knew?

She'd have to talk to them *away* from the men. But then again, everyone in this ship had also been in contact with the rift material, because of the goose eggs. She guessed that, having lived on board with the geese, Finn, Rasa, Rex, Jens and Thor were going to be safe, but Tina wasn't sure how infectious those pink globules were, and how much the other men were going to misbehave.

She made a lame excuse that she needed to rest and think, and then returned to the *Alethia* with Finn.

"They need serious help," Finn said.

Tina blew out a breath. "Yes, I'm sorry. It looks like things are even worse than we expected."

"How much can we trust the rest of the crew?"

Tina shrugged.

"Has anyone else been behaving strangely?" Finn asked.

Tina shrugged again.

"Almost everyone has been behaving strangely, but there are good reasons. Some women wanted to go back for the rest of the crew. I can understand that. Others have been paranoid. I understand that, too."

"We have to get out of here," Finn said.

"That won't solve anything. You think we carry no infection? What do you think made the geese grow funny feathers?"

"But we're not affected."

"Yet." She met his eyes. "We need knowledge and a safe place to figure out what's going on and decide what to do with that knowledge."

Arkady and his scientists. But they also needed better ships that were not damaged and preferably more and bigger ships than the *Alethia* which could only carry eight people on long-distance flights. Wherever they were going. Out of this system, as far as possible. Away from this floating death trap.

Wait a moment.

"You said something about people you had befriended?" Tina said.

"The Freerangers? I wouldn't call them friends. We just got talking."

"But they're merchants, right? And they are interested in money."

"Yes, but..."

"Invite them."

"What?"

"Invite them. I'm serious. I believe they are quite good at entering strange ships in mid-space."

"Not without damage, I think."

"I don't care."

"What are you up to? Do you really think they'll want to come here if they know what's been going on with the men?"

"From what I understand, they will probably have similar problems."

"How do you know that?"

"I don't, but Aliz said the Freeranger ships had been putting out communication in several languages. They weren't talking to the station. I'm willing to bet that they also have people acting strangely. They entered the same areas as everyone else and they bought stuff off the station. Whether that's the case doesn't matter. We're going to offer them something if they can help us."

Finn snorted. "You're going to talk to the pirates that these career military people have spent their lives fighting?"

"They're not the same type of people."

"I know, but they don't know that."

"Then we're going to tell them. Let me work on this, and we can give them my plan in the morning."

Tina was exhausted.

She entered her cabin. She'd hoped to find Rae there, but the room was empty. Rae must still be with Miriam.

Tina finally read through the notes she had received from Arkady about what they'd learned about the infection.

The process he'd called "bloom" involved the production of pink globules. It happened every few years and appeared to play a role in the infection's reproduction.

She wondered why she had never seen it at Cayelle, because she had kept cactuses for longer than a few years.

Arkady's notes also mentioned that he and his team had observed no seed being produced—the globules were just foam, even if they also spread the infection.

She had never observed this at Project Charon and wondered whether the material mimicked known life forms.

In this universe, plants flowered and set seed. She'd known

the rift material as being extremely adaptable. How likely was it that within a few reproduction cycles, it would learn to produce real seed?

There had to be a mechanism that disturbed its cycle of growth, to stop people turning into grey-skinned monsters. It was possible, because the material didn't infect everyone.

For anyone who could find that out... let's just say that many people with power and money would be interested.

It was the only way to fight the spread. The establishment at Olympus had money, but they were too self-interested to invest unless the earning potential was clear. The Force had weapons, but you couldn't fight this with weapons.

Artan wanted the infection to spread and didn't want a cure.

And the Assembly was too corrupt to be effective.

Yes, she became increasingly convinced of the way ahead.

Tina was getting hungry. She went in search of something to eat.

A few other people were in the kitchen, heating their own meals. Margot and Gisele were busy cleaning, apparently because they wanted to make sure that none of "that pink stuff" ended up in the food. They wore full-body overalls, gloves and face covering.

Tina left them to their task and gathered some food from the fridge they had designated "safe". She was about to leave when Rae came in, looking pale-faced and disturbed.

"Miriam has died."

CHAPTER TWENTY-ONE

EVERYONE in the kitchen broke out in gasps.

Margot asked, "What happened? She only had a minor cut, you said."

"How can that be?" said Cally.

"I don't know myself," Rae said. She looked truly worn out, and the first thing she did when coming into the kitchen was go to the pantry and help herself to some food. She probably hadn't eaten all day.

She spoke while stuffing bread into her mouth.

"When she came into the hospital, she was fine and talking, but she quickly went backwards. I don't know what was going on."

"Did you find any other injuries apart from the cut?" Tina asked.

"Not really."

Rae moved on to devouring the soup.

"I'm sorry for not bringing you any," Tina said.

"Don't worry about it. I'm used to it."

When Rae had finished eating, everyone insisted to go to the hospital.

Tina noticed that the two remaining men hung back. No one questioned their need to be here, but no one appeared to have asked them what they thought or knew either. Both Gerry and Stan kept giving Tina glances out of the corners of their eyes.

Oh, they definitely knew that she didn't trust them. They also didn't come with the group when they left to go to the hospital.

In the tiny emergency room, Miriam lay encased in a cubicle of glass with multiple holes for arms.

"Why is she in this thing?" Zafira asked.

"Because Rae thought she might have an infectious disease," Tina said.

They all turned around and looked at her.

"Why are you saying that? She only had a cut," Yonta said.

And even now, these women denied all the horrible possibilities. "Only a small cut" didn't make for a cause of death. There had to have been something else, and that something was likely to be the infection.

She pushed herself in the cubicle's direction, but Rae held up a gown. "Put this on first."

Tina did and then looked at Miriam through several layers of plastic.

Tina had seen several people die in her lifetime. Usually, a dead person's muscles relaxed, but Miriam's face held an anguished expression. Normally, the skin of the dead person faded, but Miriam's was red in the corner of her jaw under her ear. She was wearing a hospital gown. The bandage protruded from underneath. The skin on that arm was grey and displayed a distinctly bumpy texture. She needed to see no more. Because she had seen Vito deliberately rub his hand into the wound.

He tried to turn her into a warty pirate. Because they were a couple.

Tina faced the women, and through the visor of the mask

started her story. "I don't know how much of this you will have heard before, and I preface this by saying that we don't have all the answers either, but there are some things I must tell you. Frankly, I think the Federacy is guilty of criminal neglect by not telling you."

She then told them an abbreviated version of the current situation: that the material had come out of the rift, that it had fallen into the wrong hands either through corruption or incompetence, and that she had observed people being turned into warty creatures in the labs at Aurora.

Some women were angry.

"Why didn't you tell us before?" Yonta asked.

"Would you have believed me?"

Yonta didn't reply. They both knew the answer to that question.

But then, inevitably, the attention turned to the two remaining men.

"Are they going to turn on us, too?" Gisele said, her eyes wide.

"They may or may not, but we must act as if they will."

"We're doomed out here," Sarina said. "Why don't we just shoot ourselves?"

No one replied to that either.

"Killing ourselves would be the easy way out," Tina said. "I don't like easy ways."

"The *only* way out," Zafira said, her voice dark.

"I don't think so," Tina said. "But let me work on this. If we're going to do something, we have one chance."

"Yeah," Margot said. "At least we can eat all the food before we blow ourselves up. We only have three months' worth of curry."

No one knew how to handle that morsel of dark humour, and Tina suggested everyone tried to get some rest. As if that was easy, some women remarked.

She still waited until all the other women had left the hospital in twos and threes, crying, before speaking to Rae.

"Did you take any samples?" she asked Rae.

Rae met her eyes through the visor of the mask in a knowing look. "I did."

"Good. We'll need them. If you can, gather any blood or DNA samples from the other men and anyone else. It will be important."

Rae nodded quietly, and then said, "It seems you have a plan."

"I do, but I'm still missing a few vital components. Meanwhile, I was wondering if you would be able to contact anyone who works in astrobiology."

"What am I supposed to tell them?"

"The stuff that we know. That the pirates are deliberately infecting people. That there may be a process called bloom that helps the spread, that the infection kills some, especially women. I haven't seen a single female warty person." Except, she realised, the little girl Molly in Gandama.

She continued, "That people are being turned against their will, and that we need the assistance of any scientist who is available to help to work on a cure. It's pointless to fight the pirates. They're a symptom. The real enemy is the disease."

In Tina's limited experience, when someone died aboard a Federacy Force ship, there would be a ceremony and the body would be ejected into space.

Rae said she'd taken all her samples and was ready to hand the body over to the crew, which she did in the morning.

Tina helped wash the body, taking note that the only marks were the wound on her shoulder and a few red and grey blotches on her skin. They then dressed Miriam in a white disposable shirt they found in the hospital's stores.

She and Rae then took the body out into the mess, where the crew held a brief service.

The women from the crew belonged to several spiritual denominations, but Miriam's religious affiliation remained unclear.

Finn, Thor, Rex, Jens and Rasa were present. Tina had visited Aliz on the bridge in the morning to talk about the first part of the plan. Finn suggested that Rex, Jens and Rasa didn't need to be at this sad occasion, but Tina convinced him they did. Tina needed everyone in the same place for the first part of the plan.

Both Stan and Gerry were present at the service, although they remained at the back of the room. Tina kept an eye on them, but neither of them engaged with the women, nor did they show any grief or even speak to each other.

Conspicuously, neither asked where Vito was.

Tina suspected they would both disappear before the women could take the body out to the airlock, so she gave them a task: help transport the body, which was harder than it sounded. Rae insisted that the body remained in its anti-infection casing, and those who touched it had to wear a body suit, gloves and a visor.

Tina kept looking over her shoulder while they transported the body through the corridors.

She learned that the ship possessed one airlock that was specifically adapted for this purpose. The ship even had a catapult for making sure that bodies were ejected away from the hull so as not to collide with it.

Back when she was studying and sampling biological material from comets, she used to have nightmares about one day working with a harvesting ship taking in a comet and finding that there was a frozen body inside.

That seemed so long ago, far away in a happy time. If ever she got out of here alive, it would be one of those anecdotes one told grandchildren.

They arrived at the airlock and Yonta and Cally unfolded the slide.

But first, the men took the wrapped body out of the encasing, which they did with the help of Clodine and Rae, both of them also wearing protective suits. The four of them slid the body into the recess in the door.

Tina learned that Lisette could conduct official ceremonies.

One of the women had written a few paragraphs about Miriam's life: a loyal, fun-loving friend who would always help. Lisette's hands shook as she read the text aloud.

They were all shaken.

There was no mention of how Miriam had died, no mention of Vito at all, even if Tina understood the two had been quite close and long-term partners.

Miriam had been a cheerful person, a bit of a joker in what was otherwise a very serious environment.

Tina had never known Miriam like this, but believed the stories.

She said little, because she didn't think it was terribly appropriate, since she had known the women for such a short time.

Gerry and Stan didn't appear to care.

Most of the women eyed the men with suspicion.

They both seemed oblivious to this attention, but Tina had learned not to be so easily fooled. They would suspect that something was up the moment they would be asked to do something unusual. At least that was how they had reacted in the past.

Both men wore protective suits which made seeing the expressions on their faces and their eye-movement harder.

After Lisette finished speaking, Clodine operated the mechanism which released the body into space. By now, most of the crew members were crying. It seemed such a waste of a life.

The mood was depressing. Tina had a seed of a plan, but

she needed to do a bit more work before she could present it to the women, so to them, everything seemed lost. They were trapped on this lame ship, and the next death might well be theirs.

When the ceremony had finished, it was time for the first part of Tina's plan.

Before Gerry and Stan could disappear—they had already taken off their visors—she asked them to take the protective transport casing to the washroom, so that Rae could clean the inside to minimise the risk of further infection.

"Why us?" Stan asked.

"You're big and strong men, and Rae is only small and not heavy enough to take the case by herself."

Rae was not aware that Tina had held a discussion with Aliz about this, and she started protesting that she could very well move the casing by herself, because it wasn't terribly heavy, only awkward.

But Tina said that the men could make themselves useful that way.

Gerry commented that he wasn't a message boy.

"It's fine, I'll do it," Rae said.

"No, they will do it," Tina insisted.

"He's right, we're not here to be messenger boys," Stan said.

"Look, we are all doing things we are not trained to do. It's necessary, so you do it."

They mumbled, but eventually took off with the case.

Tina glanced at Aliz.

Phew. That had been a close thing.

Now for the final move.

They waited until both men had entered the laundry block, and then Aliz activated the control. The door clicked shut.

Several of the women glanced at each other.

"Did you just lock the door on them?" Lisette said.

"I did," Aliz said.

Gerry came to the door and banged on it. His face was red behind the little round window.

"Let us out. Open this door."

"Why did you do that?" Zafira asked.

"You know why," Tina said. "I don't like it either, but we have to protect ourselves. I can't explain to them what we're doing, because then they will flee inside the ship, and it's big enough for them to evade us for such a long time that we'll spend all our resources trying to catch them, and it may be too late. They will sabotage us if we give them half a chance."

No one protested.

But Sarina asked, "How long do you want to lock them up for?"

"Until we're safe. We must restrain them until we're sure they won't turn on us as well."

"But can't you at least explain it to them?"

Gerry was still banging on the door, his face red and eyes panicked.

"I don't like this," Lisette said. "You tricked them. They've done nothing."

"Yet," Tina said. "Or anything that we can prove. I don't like it either, but I don't want to end up like Miriam."

No one could say anything in response to that.

Tina went to the door. "Be quiet. We will bring food. We'll make sure you're comfortable."

Gerry yanked at the door handle. "Let us out. We've done nothing!"

The door rattled with his efforts.

"Let us out! Hey, let us out!"

She turned around to a group of anguished faces. However, no one protested. No one spoke to Tina either. Would she prefer to be justified in her caution? Or would she prefer that she was too cautious, nothing happened and the crew turned against her? Either option was terrible.

How they were going to supply the men was another question. She had selected the laundry section because only one door led into it, but that meant they would have to supply the men via that door as well, and that might be dangerous.

"That was one of the most terrible things I've had to do to someone who is not an enemy," she said to Aliz as they made their way back to the mess.

Aliz said, "I hope you know what you're doing."

"I have no idea. I'm making it up as I go."

CHAPTER TWENTY-TWO

THE ENTIRE EPISODE left Tina feeling so exhausted that even Rex asked if she was all right. She wasn't all right, not really, but there would be no rest until a plan was sorted, approved by the crew and put in motion.

There was no time to feel sorry for herself.

After a quick bite to eat, Tina said everyone should go to bed.

People left the mess, but Tina held Finn back.

"I would like to talk to you for a bit," she said.

They went a little way down the passage they would follow to go down to the docks under the excuse that they needed to retrieve something from the *Alethia.*

"We need to get out of here," Finn said in a low voice once they were out of sight of the others.

"You tell me. But I hope you're not suggesting that we leave these women with all their problems?"

"Well, I didn't mean that at all."

"Good. Because now I have my two children safe and together, I'm going to make sure both of them will stay safe."

"And you have an idea how?"

"An idea. But I need all the help I can get to make it work."

"I guess that's where I come in? I hope you don't think I have bottomless pits of money, because I don't. When I left, my family actually—"

"Finn, stop it."

"Stop what?"

"I don't want to hear your bellyaching about your poor family and how bad your life is."

"I wasn't going to—"

"Yes, you were. I don't want money from your family. Yes, I guess I do, but I don't want *charity* from them, and I don't want it until much later in the plan. I want you to sweet-talk these Freerangers into providing transport for us."

"You—what?" He laughed.

"This ship is lame and isn't going to take us anywhere. We don't have enough crew to either fix or fly it. We need to go back to the station to get Arkady and the other scientists, and then we need to go to a safe location elsewhere."

"And where is this magical safe location?"

"That's what we need the Freerangers for."

"Wait—I thought they were going to provide transport. I can ask them that, as long as we pay."

"We have no money, and can offer them none, but I'm going to offer them the biggest prize of all."

"Which is?"

"Legitimacy."

"What?"

"Legitimacy and a guaranteed income—if they help us gather the people and equipment we need to defeat this infection that will stop the senseless war and will stop us becoming horrible, tentacled monsters."

He gaped at her.

She said, "Because no one seems to be interested in actually fighting this stuff. Because it's also powerful in other ways. And makes them lots of money."

He was still gaping, so she added, "Because they're after me because I have a lot of the pieces already, and me publishing that paper on the cactuses made them realise that."

Finn seemed so dumbfounded that he had nothing to say.

"So what I want to know is if you're prepared to stick out your neck and help us, because you know, you could be very useful, but I'm guessing that it won't make you terribly popular with the crowd at Olympus. I'm betting on the fact that you're not terribly popular with them already."

He blew out a long breath and finally said something.

"Nothing like a motherly type to thoroughly whup your ass."

"I'm not a motherly type."

"Are you kidding? You're something like fifteen years older than me, and you're exactly like my mother. And you're telling me to stop dicking around, get a grip and get my head out of my rear end."

"I didn't say anything like—"

"Yes, you did. In fact, you've said nothing else since I came on this trip. Everything you say, whether you comment on my family or my sorry shambles of a marriage, is some form of 'get your act together, spoilt rich boy'."

"I never say that."

"No, you never used the words, but that look in your eyes is clearer than words. And let's be honest, I am a spoilt rich boy. I have no idea what the fuck I'm doing. I could blame people for not telling me, but it was probably because I wasn't listening and I couldn't hear them because my ears were full of the rumbling of my own gas because I had my head so far up my own arse that I could see out my mouth. And I don't know what the fuck I'm doing, and everyone goes like *Oh are you that*

Kaspari? when they hear my name and expect me to be some sort of—I don't know—magic business playboy."

"It's not easy being rich."

"I'm not rich. My family is."

"Yes, and if I were you, I'd use the batshit out of that, not try to run from it."

He looked at her, wide-eyed as if he wanted to say, "What? Actually talk to them?"

"You're a failure at being an average Joe, so how about you start being Finn Kaspari?"

He stared at her. "And do what?"

"The things I'm going to ask you to do, and I need you to do them while being a Kaspari, while being confident, swaggering, blunt, convincing. Throw money around, threaten to withdraw it, whatever."

"You have a very high opinion of what my family does."

"That's the impression they give me. I don't care. Do whatever you've grown up learning to do."

"And what is it you want me to achieve?"

"Get those Freerangers over here. Get them to go to the station to pick up Arkady, then get them to give us a safe haven to do our work. Promise them a share of profits if we find a cure. Whatever."

"Huh."

And then he said nothing for a while.

"There's only one problem with that."

"And that is?"

"You may find it difficult to get a military crew to accept help from Freerangers. Most of them are still of the opinion that the Freerangers and the pirates are the same group."

"Yes." Tina sighed. It would be hard, especially since the ship carried technology that Aliz and the flight crew had sworn to keep out of enemy hands. They would blow up the ship before letting someone else get their hands on it. And Freerangers might trigger the *someone else* response.

"Well, we'll have to—"

Finn spread his hands. "What's this about we? You're the one who's good at talking. I know the Freerangers and can talk to them. I don't know this Arkady and you know what the military thinks of me. You'll have to convince them."

"Well, I don't think the scientists will need much convincing. I assume that all the researchers are still on Aurora Station. Whatever they're doing, they will like going to a safe place, because living on Aurora is like living in a prison, and things are getting worse and worse. Arkady and the other people were very nervous. They've been doing some really excellent work on this disease. I could use them. I need them. This type of research needs a large team of scientists. We need to start up a lab and we need to fill it with as many scientists as possible. We can't wait for the Federacy give us money and projects. How about we create our own solutions? The Federacy is not interested in solving this crisis. We have seen the levels of corruption in their ranks. I don't think they are interested in solving this problem at all, not when they're being paid money to support interests that benefit the pirates."

"That leaves the crew of this ship kind of in the wild."

"Yeah. No matter how much these women consider that they're part of an honourable organisation, the organisation doesn't give a crap about them. It's going to be hard to get them to admit that and accept what they can do to fix it."

CHAPTER TWENTY-THREE

TINA LOOKED around the circle of people gathered at the bridge.

A meeting of the ship's crew only, Aliz had said, so Finn, Thor, Jens, Rex and Rasa weren't present.

"So, to repeat, you suggest we go to the station, pick up these scientists, and then take this heavily armed military ship to a pirate stronghold and work with them?" Yonta said. "Can anyone tell me why this isn't a ridiculous idea?"

Framed like that, no one had an appetite to answer that question. Yonta had been defensive ever since Tina had started talking about her plan. Tina was especially annoyed at how she said the word "scientists". She was highly tempted to ask if Yonta was sure that she was the smartest person in all of inhabited space.

But she suspected that at least some of the crew agreed with Yonta.

"That is my suggestion," Tina said. "I present it to you for comments."

"It's never going to be acceptable," Yonta said. "Worse, it's an insult to all those who have lost their lives fighting the pirates.

How are we expected to trust people who we've been fighting for years? Even if we can pay them to get us out of here, and I doubt their ability to do that."

"That is just the point I'm trying to make you understand. You haven't been fighting *these* people. Artan and his people infiltrated the group we know as pirates. We need a new word for them. They're not the same groups. You've been fighting pirates, not Freerangers."

"Huh, they're all the same to me. Rabble. If this distinction was so important, people would have pointed it out before."

"No, people don't care. Because the Freerangers are a group on the margins of society, by their own choice."

"Because they're criminals, smugglers and cheats."

"There *are* some of those, but not all of them. But because they're on the margins of society, they're also poorly monitored, which is also why the mutant pirates could successfully infiltrate them."

"And you want us to give these people access to a highly advanced warship that we have sworn to protect?"

"This ship is lame and not going anywhere in its current condition."

She met Aliz's eyes. Never mind Yonta's bluster, it was Aliz she needed to win over, because Aliz was bridge crew and they would go down with the ship before allowing it to fall into the hands of anyone who could be seen as the enemy.

"Let us talk to this group at the very least," Tina said. "They're not far from here. Finn spoke to them at the station. They're merchants. They are the traditional type, with shipworlds."

"Those people have nothing we want," Zafira said. "We need trained crew."

"We don't want extra people? We don't want a working ship? We don't want people who can help us survive or avoid becoming warty monsters? Can we finally agree that everyone who has spent any time in the labs is likely to be a risk to us? Do we want Miriam to have died in vain?"

"It's crazy," Yonta said.

But everyone looked at Aliz, because she had said very little in this discussion so far. And she continued to not say very much at all, but sat staring into space, a frown on her face.

"None of us want to die," Tina continued. "We will die if we stay here and do nothing. Artan's pirates will mop us up when they get half a chance. They'll probably do so in passing, on the way to doing something important, while laughing at us. They'll squash us like a cockroach. We've already seen that other Federacy ships are neither in the position nor willing to come to our aid. They think we're infected and our systems compromised. We might well be. I understand you have your orders not to let this ship fall into enemy hands—"

"'Protect it with your lives,' were the Admiral's words," Aliz said. "He said them to me and the other flight crew, all of whom are now missing or dead. I don't like the thought of betraying my orders or the memory of my fellow crew."

There were some nods at that.

Aliz continued, "I agree with Tina. If we do nothing, we will achieve nothing except our own slow and excruciating deaths, from infection, from fights with each other, from hunger, or from being invaded by pirates when they feel like it and whenever they can do so for our maximum embarrassment and exposure. We could be all heroic and blow ourselves up before we get to that stage, but I also agree that it will achieve nothing, not even our martyrdom. We're already lost to the Federacy."

"OK, then we try to do something ourselves," Yonta said. "Crazy as it sounds, if you want the scientists, we can get the scientists and start our own research project, or whatever."

Aliz said, "We don't have suitable ships to go back to the station. We can't go with this ship and the fighters don't have the right docking capabilities, besides being too small to carry passengers."

"What about your ship?" Yonta looked at Tina.

"It doesn't carry many people, it's known to station authorities, it's not a merchant ship and may attract suspicion. On top of that, we need Gerry's help to get the ship out. And if we don't get these scientists, we won't have anyone to work with for the next stage of the plan. Getting out of here is not the aim of my plan. It's a prerequisite. But whatever we do afterwards is what's going to make the difference. We don't have enough people for that stage of the plan. We need those scientists and their knowledge."

"We have Rae."

"Yes, we do, but solving problems of this kind requires huge numbers of people."

"And you suggest we use pirate-owned facilities to do this?"

"Freeranger," Tina said. "We must get used to not calling these people pirates. They're Freerangers."

"I don't care. I don't want to have anything to do with them," Yonta said. "They're rabble motivated only by money."

"Same here," Cally said. "They're just waiting out there so that they can pounce on the ship and sell it to the highest bidder."

"Then we're back at the position where everyone dies." Tina spread her hands. "In that case, if you're too stubborn, I ask that you let the *Alethia* go, so that we can be on our way."

"Mum, no!" Evelle said, her eyes wide.

"You're free to come. I've spent enough time in the Force to know that everyone is disposable. They don't care about you in their offices at Olympus. They're not worth dying for. We don't have to do exactly what I propose, but we have to do *something*. If you don't want to try anything and are going to just sit here and wait until help turns up, I'm going. I have the responsibility for my own people and no allegiance to this ship or to any military superiors."

Evelle was looking at her, her expression anguished.

Tina didn't want to leave Evelle. She desperately didn't want that, but the situation was getting worse and slipping out of her control.

Then someone said in a clear voice, "Let's just be sensible about this."

It was Rae.

As Tina had noticed earlier, people took note when she spoke.

"We don't all share the same loyalties," Rae continued.

"Huh, tell me something I didn't know," Yonta said.

"It bears repeating. It also bears repeating that we all want to survive. And we are arguing because we are afraid. We should stop being afraid."

"What do you mean?" Several women called out at the same time.

"Yes, I know it sounds strange to call a group of tough military people afraid. But we are afraid of consequences to ourselves if we take action that might displease our superiors or that would contradict our orders. But we're at a point where our predicament is no longer covered by orders. Every single one of our options looks bad. But we forget one thing: history. History cannot be told if there is no one to tell it. If we don't survive, the memory of our capture will be forgotten, because we will be 'missing in action' according to the Federacy. No one will know that pirates were waiting for us when we were separated from the main fleet. No one will know that we were captured, taken into Aurora Station, and that some of us were deliberately infected. No one will investigate why the pirate fleet knew where we were and where we were going, and no one will question where our mates are."

She looked around, her eyes fierce.

"So for the memory of all the crew who died, we must survive. Going down with the ship is ridiculous and wasteful, and is exactly what the upper command wants, so that they can turn us into martyrs and sweep under the carpet all the stuff that led to our deaths. I vote that rather than fighting each other and bickering over what to do, we should get out of here by whatever means available to us, grab all the people that we think can help us, and take them to a safe place so that we can make sure that our story is heard."

Aliz added, "I've already said this so many times, but we can't fly the ship with the current crew. I don't really want to abandon the ship near a pirate base, and honestly, I don't think a corrupt upper command is worth our lives. You deserve better than that. Your families deserve better than that. If it's all the same with you, I'll be telling Tina to do what's necessary to get out of here."

All the women were silent. It seemed they had never accepted Tina's leadership, but they accepted the superior voice of the captain.

CHAPTER TWENTY-FOUR

TINA SENT A MESSAGE TO FINN, *We're on.*

He'd seemed a bit put out when the crew requested he didn't attend the meeting, and she hoped he was ready to put it behind him.

Judging by the look on his face, she wasn't sure that he had. She was also reminded that he hadn't been overly keen on using his contacts with the Freerangers.

This part of the plan seemed shaky and could fall apart without notice. If the Freerangers weren't interested, who else could they contact? From what she understood, there were several groups of Freerangers in the area. Maybe they could try another group, if Finn had a contact for them.

Finn asked Aliz if he could contact the family from the controls of the *Alethia* but she said it would confuse the people.

On the other hand, if the communication came from the *Alethia*, it would be clear that Finn was involved.

Most of all, Tina noticed Finn was incredibly self-conscious and insecure. He didn't like people listening in. He got nervous about people recording stuff.

But he set his unease aside and used the contact he'd been

given from the communication hub of the *Manila*. By this time, only Tina, Aliz and Evelle were still on the bridge. Aliz was past the end of her shift, but in her position, Tina would also have kept going.

While the three of them crowded around the communication bay, the light from the screen gilding their faces, Tina thought about how utterly exhausted the others looked and that it would be impossible to keep going like this.

The signal connected.

A crackle and beep came from the loudspeakers.

Finn said, "This is David from the private vessel *Alethia* on board the Starfighter *Manila*. I want to speak with Clementine of the Shipworld Mara."

Of course he had used his second ID.

"Shipworld Mara speaking. What is your business?"

The voice was formal. A man, Tina thought. Unlikely to answer to the name Clementine.

"We're on board the Starfighter *Manila*. We have a proposition."

"We are not currently selling any food or other essentials. If you want to trade non-food items for food or ship supplies, please be advised that we can only do so to agencies that have signed a needs-based distribution agreement."

"No, it's not about that. I would like to speak with Clementine."   .

"Your name was?"

"David Metz. We met at the station. She gave me this contact."

Some scuffling noises followed, and a moment later, a woman's voice sounded from the loudspeakers. "Yes?"

Not someone who sounded terribly friendly. "Is that her?" Tina mouthed to Finn. This was going to be very dicey.

Finn took in a visible deep breath. "You will probably remember meeting me at the station's docks where we were both waiting to pick up ship crew who had been stranded at the station. I introduced myself as David Metz."

"Oh, yes. We haven't been able to trace that name yet."

"I have a proposition to you."

"Not so quick. I can see you're on board that warship. What are you doing there?"

"There are only a handful of crew left on board. The ship is as good as dead. We came on board and they simply surrendered."

Aliz's eyes widened.

Finn continued, "We're acting as private citizens. We have plans for this ship, but we don't have enough people to fly it. The ship's crew are admin officers and other folk with knowledge useless for flying the ship. I'm an engineer, but I can't look after the ship by myself. The main engine is damaged. It needs to go into dock, but I don't want that piece of shit at Aurora to get his hands on it. The engine can operate at fifty percent, so if you can lend us two or more ships that we can use to tow us, that would be ideal."

"That ship is enormous. Where do you want to go?"

"Wherever you can take us. To a place we can fix this thing."

"What about the Federacy nutsos? What are you going to say to them when they turn up with their armies?"

"There won't be any. The crew tried to beg for help, but no one is game to come. They've been abandoned."

"What about the pirates?"

"Heh, do you want to see the rockets on this baby?"

"OK. If we help, we want a share of the sale value."

"Oh no, I'm not selling this baby."

"Then how do you expect to pay for the service?"

"I'll pay. You'll find out why when you come here. There are further work contracts and rewards involved. My boss will only tell you in person."

The woman hesitated.

"How do I know you're not trying to trick us?"

"If I wanted to trick you, I would do it differently. Think of it, we are on the bridge of a large warship. If we had the capability and the people, we would blast our way out of this place and I wouldn't be offering to trade with you. There are no tricks."

She hesitated again.

"I want your guarantee that we will be allowed to approach the ship without danger. We have families on board."

"I know. I saw them, right?"

"And if we come, I expect a fair negotiation, and I expect to be allowed to leave if we so choose."

"I guarantee that, but I can also guarantee you you will not be interested in leaving without us. I know that you have a nose for good business."

"Just so you understand: conducting business is our thing. We don't pick sides or fight wars. And we have nothing to do with the criminals that occupy the station. They may pretend that they're our allies, and a few rogue shipworlds seemed to have joined them, but we are the traditional Freeranger Mara family, and we have nothing to do with them. We are traders and do nothing that goes against our laws. We don't always obey your laws, but we adhere to the basic laws of human respect and freedom. We don't kill people, we don't infect people. We don't cheat, we don't lie, and we don't keep prisoners."

"I understand. You may approach and we will allow you to leave safely."

Finn signed off.

Aliz blew out a breath and shook her head, clearly conflicted about her orders in relation to this big, dangerous and secretive ship.

Tina thought it wise not to say anything, and Finn didn't say anything either.

But Evelle said, "So, you're really from *that* Kaspari family?"

Tina glanced at Finn and had to restrain herself not to laugh.

Finn said, "Yes, I'm *that* Kaspari, and if they want bluff and bluster, that's what we do. Apparently, it's all I'm good for."

"I think you're a half-decent engineer, too," Tina said.

Evelle frowned at both of them. The conversation went over her head.

The Freerangers sent a scheduled time for arrival, which meant there was time for the women to attend to other tasks, such as to bring food to the men.

Tina made sure that Rex, Rasa and Jens had enough to eat and were comfortable. Then she sent them with Thor to the *Alethia*. On the way, she quietly told Thor to get ready for any possibility, which included the ship having to depart the dock of the *Manila* at short notice.

Then she paid a visit to the storeroom where Vito was tied up.

Rae was in there, dressed up in protective gear, attempting to put a line in his arm to feed him.

"He won't eat in any other way," she said when she noticed Tina at the door. She looked frazzled and tired, not made better by Vito because he would not keep his arms still.

Rae grew frustrated with him. "If I don't get this into your arm, you will die within days."

Vito mumbled something through the tape that covered his mouth and that, judging by the number of moustache hairs stuck to it, looked to have been ripped off and reapplied several times. His eyes were wide, his face sheened with sweat.

The skin on his arms had broken out in raw and red bumps. They had to be itchy.

"That doesn't look comfortable," Tina said.

"No. It's painful and itchy. I've taken samples," Rae said through the visor. "I think he is much worse than we realise."

Tina didn't ask about the usual things, such as recovery and his outlook. There would be no recovery until they figured out the cause of the mutation, and he was probably too far gone, anyway. They'd have to make some hard decisions once he mutated enough to grow tentacles.

"What about the other two?" Tina asked.

"I visited them about an hour ago," Rae said. "They are doing much better. At least they are still talking to each other."

But when Tina got to the laundry, it was to find Cally and Sarina at the little window that looked into the room. Heavy thuds sounded from the other side of the door, and when Tina entered the hallway, both women cast a nervous glance over their shoulders.

"What's going on?" Tina asked.

"Stan is angry because Gerry escaped and we shut the door before he could get out as well," Cally said.

"Gerry escaped? How can that be?" Tina asked. "Did someone open the door?"

"Of course we did. We need to open the door to give them food. Gerry overwhelmed Clodine and took off into the ship."

Damn, that was just what they could use while the Freerangers were approaching with their only chance to get out of here safely. Finn had told them nothing about the infected men, but she could only imagine what would happen if Gerry attacked the Freeranger delegation.

"Is Clodine all right?" Tina asked. They couldn't afford to lose any more people.

"Yes, but she was livid. She went to the store to get tools. She said she was going to cut a piece out of this door and make a flap, so we can give them food without having to go in. She said she'd bolt the door shut, and they'd have to clean up their own floating shit."

That would only work in the short term. If Stan really wanted to create trouble in the laundry, it would be easy.

Connections for water and electricity presented endless possibilities for mischief. Would it be possible to isolate the laundry and turn off all power?

"We have to find Gerry," Tina said.

Cally nodded, her face grave.

Find him and tie him up like Vito.

Tina felt sick at the thought. The men were ill, and they needed care. Even Gandama produced better circumstances for an infected person. Likely, locking them up only increased the men's anger.

"Where is Gerry likely to go first?" Tina asked.

"My guess: anywhere he can find food."

So they went to the kitchen, but they came too late: Gerry had already been there. The place was a mess, with items pulled out of the storage compartments and floating in the central space. Packages had been broken and things ripped out of the cupboards.

Food containers and cutlery floated around the place.

"He must have been looking for something," Cally said.

Margot said, "If he was after food, he would have taken this stuff with him. There is plenty of food in this place. He's just made a mess for the sake of making a mess."

Tina said, "Well, we'll have to clean this up before the Freerangers arrive. Any idea where we're going to meet them?"

"As close as possible to the place where they enter the ship," Aliz said in her earpiece. "I don't know where that is going to be yet. Just stow the stuff so it doesn't get lost or get into the vents and come this way. I spotted movement in the A sector."

The ship's two long corridors ran the length of the hull, and several side corridors connected the two. The kitchen and mess compartment lay off one crossbeam. Another major connection between the two sides of the ship lay closer to the stern.

While Tina helped retrieve most rogue items to return

them to the storage compartments in the kitchen, Aliz shared her screen.

Tina saw it too, a dark figure hiding in an alcove. She zoomed out. He was in the corridor that led to the docks.

She gave the *Alethia* a warning. "Finn, he's coming your way."

Aliz said, "He can't get into the docks. The safety doors are shut."

"We can trap him where the door closes the passage," Cally said.

Tina followed Cally and Sarina into the corridor.

Aliz turned on the lights to maximum strength.

Ahead, the lone figure came out of hiding. It was Gerry indeed.

He pulled himself along, using the handholds on the walls. Tina and her group followed. He was quick.

He arrived at the metal door that separated the passage from the maintenance section and turned to the control panel.

"Do you think he can open it?" Sarina asked.

Cally didn't answer that.

"He needs to go through to reach Vito." As Tina said this, she suspected that reaching Vito was why Gerry was here.

That couldn't be allowed to happen. They had to stop him.

Cally gestured the women into an alcove with a glass-fronted cabinet at the end. She held her ID card up to the lock on a panel on the wall. A light flickered. She opened the door.

The cabinet contained a couple of concertinaed boards with card sleeves. Each held an access card. What an old-fashioned thing.

Cally took out a card from a slot that said *weapons depot*.

"We have to stop him, regardless of the consequences," she said in a low voice to Tina and Sarina. "If that means we have to kill him, that's what we will do." She stuck the card in her pocket. "We need to arm ourselves before we face him."

When they returned to the hallway, there was no sign of Gerry. Worse, the metal security door to the maintenance area had been forced open far enough for a person to pass.

"Shit, he knew how to open that door," Cally said.

Cally first led the group past the weapons store. Clodine caught up with them, sporting a rip in her shirt, but no other signs of injury. Since she usually worked in this part of the ship, she chose and distributed the weapons. Fireseeds, a Q-blaster, which she took herself. Tina got a Fireseed303, the latest model.

Clodine shut and locked the depot's door with the words, "I hope we won't need these."

That went without saying.

Tina just hoped that trouble would stay away from the *Alethia*, and that Rex, Rasa, Jens and Thor would stay inside. Hopefully Aliz would have told them what was going on.

They set out in the direction of the room where they had tied up Vito. His protests echoed in the hallway, in an anguished voice that disturbed Tina.

These men never asked to be subjected to this infection. They had been loyal crew members. They didn't deserve this.

Gerry was nowhere to be seen.

They then checked the docking hall, but everything was quiet there, too.

The doors to the *Alethia* were closed, and the remaining fighter craft hung in their positions, their canopies still safely locked.

Where had Gerry gone?

"He's got to be somewhere around here," Sarina said.

On the other side of the docking hall was a short passage leading to several rooms full of equipment and supplies needed for aircraft and habitat operations maintenance.

Wait.

Of course.

"He will be in here," Tina said, pointing ahead. "He's collecting tools to get out of here, get into the craft, or poison us."

"Damn," Cally said. "The chemical stores."

Tina first entered the passage, pulling herself along the wall.

Sounds of ripping packaging came from somewhere down the end.

"We know you're here," she said.

The ripping sounds continued.

"Come out and we won't harm you. We're armed."

Again, he didn't reply, so Tina continued. Cally and Sarina were close behind her. Cally handed Tina a safety gas mask. Tina stopped to pull it over her face. It was hot inside the goggles and the straps got in her way. The contraption held a battery for the fan and a small air tank with leads. She turned on the fan to stop the visor fogging up.

They entered a large storeroom.

A muffled male voice called, "Come and get me if you dare!"

Gerry came out from behind a storage rack, wearing an environment suit with a visor and breathing apparatus, dragging a large yellow drum along with him. A warning label declared the content to be poisonous.

"Let that thing go now," Clodine said, gesturing with her Q-blaster.

She was much better trained in fighting in Zero-G combat than Tina and kept the weapon trained on him while he floated through the open space and she hung upside down in the doorway.

He stopped himself floating by kicking against the edge of a storage compartment.

"Do you think you can stop me with that thing?" he said and laughed. "You know what this is? Sulphuric acid. If I throw it in the vat with disinfectant over there, it will go kaboom. If I throw it on the heater over there, it will produce foul gas. If you shoot it—"

"Why, Gerry? What have we done to harm you?" Tina asked.

His head turned to search briefly before locating her. Confused, she thought, but it was hard to see because his face hid behind the visor.

"Why are you doing this? You're hurting the people who care about you."

"Care about me? They locked up Vito."

"Vito attacked someone, and she died."

Tina couldn't see much of his face through the visor, but he seemed to hesitate. "She is dead?" He sounded confused.

"Yes. Do you know her name? Say her name."

"Why didn't you tell me that she is dead?"

"We told you. You even came to the service, remember?"

"You didn't tell me. You didn't!" This was not going well. His voice rose into a shriek.

He undid the lid of the yellow container. The pouring spout that extended had anti-spill protection, but he held the drum upside down and shook it violently. Globs of fluid drifted out, issuing poisonous vapour.

"Everyone get out of here," Cally yelled.

They all made for the door. Sarina managed to push it shut before Gerry could follow.

But this was not an atmosphere proof security door, and it didn't close hermetically. It also couldn't be locked and would only divert Gerry briefly. He was already at the door.

The women sped to the point where the passage opened into the maintenance hall.

Cally was pulling on gloves. "Make sure you cover your skin because if you touch that stuff, it will burn."

Clodine had hit the air quality alarm.

Tina pulled in the air tank that trailed her through the air.

She turned the valve at the top. She found a set of gloves stuffed inside a recess in the strap that dangled from the tank that was for tying it around one's waist. She put them on and strapped the tank on.

Aliz yelled in her ear because she wanted to know why the atmosphere alarms were going off at the bridge.

Gerry came through the passage, still shaking the container. Poisonous globules floated in the hallway, in the rooms, near the ceiling, on the floors, giving off their vapour.

"Don't shoot, the stuff is flammable," Tina called out.

Gerry laughed, yelling inside his mask.

"He's gone mad," Cally said.

This was not going to end well.

They couldn't use their weapons as long as he carried the container.

The first door on the left led into another store room. It contained stacks of big and heavy crates secured on a metal grid that cris-crossed the room. Those crates were too big to be of use—but wait.

One crate contained pressurised cylinders. If, by chance, they contained something more useful than flammable or explosive stuff, like oxygen, she could use those. Tina checked the closest label. Helium. Perfect.

She pulled the tank out of the rack. A couple of clips held it in place, but it slid out relatively easily. She held it up, the bottom pointed at the door.

Cally appeared to understand what she wanted.

When Gerry came in, she opened the top valve on the cylinder. Gas shot out with a hiss. The cylinder flew from Tina's hands. The force of the escaping gas flung her backwards.

The stream of gas escaped the valve at an angle, tilting the cylinder sideways. Gerry took a full hit from the wayward projectile. He flew backwards. The cylinder's height was greater than the width of the door and it clanged into the door frame.

Gerry flew out the door, across the hallway, and smacked into the wall with a thud that made the metal shudder.

Cally and Sarina sped over. They pushed him against the wall to subdue him and used a roll of tape to tie his hands together and then tie his feet to his hands so he resembled an insect caught in a spider web. He couldn't move.

They locked him into another maintenance room.

Phew. That was a close thing.

Tina was hot inside the mask, but they had to wait until the poisonous gas cloud that Gerry had released had dissipated. But Sarina said the ship's ventilation could deal with it, precisely because this was a chemicals store.

CHAPTER TWENTY-FIVE

WELL, phew, that was close.

"We have to make sure they don't escape anymore," Clodine said.

"I really don't like this," Sarina said. "It feels to me like we should offer them help. They're sick. They're not criminals."

"I don't like it either," Tina said. "But the fact that they're sick won't change the other fact that they attacked us and tried to sabotage the ship. If we get out of here, and if we can get my project started, and if we find a cure, they will be the first to receive treatment."

Of course there was no guarantee they could find treatment in time, but it wouldn't be for her lack of trying.

Aliz called for the crew to be alert. The Freeranger ships were approaching. Nobody yet knew how the Freerangers were going to board the *Manila* but they needed to prepare, because there was no way that Vito, Gerry or Stan, or their condition, should be part of the negotiations.

Tina returned to the bridge, where both Aliz and Evelle were at the controls. Most of the other women had gathered at the central holdfast bar that crossed the bridge space, watching the large screen in front of Aliz.

The Freerangers were approaching with a small fleet of five ships. Two of them were small, probably shuttles they would use to visit the station. The third was slightly bigger, and the last two were quite sizeable.

They were odd-looking things, cylinder shapes that were mostly engine. The habitat sat at the front of the ship, shaped like a disk attached to the rest of the ship by a central pole. Tina guessed the disk rotated around the pole in mid-flight, although it wasn't moving now.

She had never seen this type of ship before. It reminded her of the picture in school history books of the very first interstellar ships.

"I can't believe those old models are still operating." Yonta's voice came from the loudspeakers.

She was not at the bridge, but was following the action from her control room in the docks, in case the Freerangers wanted to come in that way.

"I've seen these people use ships older than those," Cally said. "I've seen ships without revolving habitat, the traditional tube shape with panels on the outside where you could see the rivets in the surface. It's at least sixty years since that building style was abandoned."

Yonta said, "Look at the size of the engines on these things relative to the size of the ship. I hate to think how much fuel they use."

"Burning fuel is a physical reaction," Aliz said. "If you can tinker with the engine so that it burns more efficiently, or you get a more efficient fuel, the size of the engine doesn't really matter, it's about how much fuel you burn."

"But the mass of the ship will matter," Cally said.

"All these old ships are very large, and they are built for safety, not for speed. Besides, unless you have anti gravity couches, it's the fragility of the inhabitants that determines the maximum acceleration, not the structure or the size of the engine."

"Thanks for the physics lesson," Cally said and laughed.

The Freeranger fleet had come closer, and the time for banter was over. It was time for business.

Did the Freerangers want the docking door to open, Aliz asked them.

They said they didn't. They said they were going to use an emergency airlock close to the *Manila*'s residential area. Aliz said she'd disable the one-way lock on the outer door.

"We'll gather in the mess," Aliz said to the crew. Margot said she'd prepare the room. Tina wondered how much of the mess Gerry had made was still floating around.

The fact that the Freerangers weren't entering through the docking area let Finn and Thor off the hook, because they didn't need to secure the *Alethia* or help with the boarding.

It also avoided the issue of strangers crossing that area which contained sensitive equipment, as well as the remote possibility of the Freerangers noticing the three prisoners locked up in the ship's utility rooms adjacent to the docks.

The Freeranger ships came closer than Aliz was comfortable with, then they shot out something that attached to the hull with a clang. It was some kind of sucker cup with a cable attached, Yonta said, because she had a clearer view.

Then they let two people out of the ship at the end of the cable. The airlock door was on the shadow side of the Freeranger ship, but the tiny figures were visible by the light that reflected off the hull of the *Manila*. Both clipped their tethers onto the cable and sailed through space to the *Manila*. Yonta's outside cameras picked them up for the last part.

Their environment suits were hard-shelled, with mechanical joints that were probably operated from the bulky battery pack that sat on top of the air tanks on their backs.

Aliz laughed. "I didn't even know these outfits were still in use."

Tina remembered having seen those types of suits—in a museum.

But the two inhabitants of the suits navigated the outside of the *Manila*, detached the cable, which then allowed their ship to move away again—much to Aliz's relief—and entered the emergency airlock.

A moment later they came into the ship.

"That's how easy it is to board ships," Aliz said. "Sometimes you cannot help but wonder what we've got this whole military installation for."

"They would never get this close unless we let them," Cally said.

"Yeah, and you needed to unlock the door."

But trained ship crew would understand. A spearheaded attack by a small entity was the fear of the captain of every large ship.

Tina remembered how in her training an officer had mentioned how a small party with crude but unconventional methods could do a huge amount of damage to a large ship. Because basically, they were people and people were smart and thought of a thousand different ways to circumvent problems.

The officer had said, "If they're hungry, angry and keen, they're going to have much a greater motivation than personnel who are paid to do jobs and who, in order to keep those jobs, need to satisfy ten layers of bureaucracy before they can act. Remember that. These people are dangerous. They've got zero long-term staying power, but can cause a lot of damage. Underestimating them is a dumb move."

The two people who came out of the airlock not much later were a man and a woman. The man was easily the youngest of the two, perhaps in his late twenties. The woman had greying hair, tied in a long plait that floated behind her in weightlessness.

Underneath their suits, they wore blue garments that looked like the robes they had worn in the station. Bands made from stretchy fabric around the arms and legs held the garments in place.

It looked quite comfortable because the fabric ballooned out around the joints and the wearer would have plenty of freedom to move.

Both Freerangers were fairly dark-skinned, but that could be because of exposure to artificial sunlight.

They introduced themselves as Clementine and Rubiano Mara. They moved in Zero-G with confidence. If they were intimidated by the number of military uniforms facing them, they didn't show it. Everyone had come to the meeting, even Aliz and Evelle.

Tina started by explaining to the two visitors who she was and about her history. She told them about having worked for the Federacy, having left when she became disillusioned, her role in the research about the rift material, and her possible role in the spread of the infection.

She explained why she had come back to space after having spent fifteen years at Cayelle, and how she had found the world a rather different place from the one she had left. She spoke about her family, about having found Evelle, and still on the lookout for what happened to her husband, although she hastened to say she was not interested in joining up with him.

"You maybe puzzled why I am telling you all of this, but you need a proper understanding of where I'm coming from. I am a biological scientist foremost, and although the Federacy has tried in the past, they couldn't buy my loyalty, because I make my decisions based on results, and we cannot buy results. To that extent, it is important you know the other members of our party."

She gestured to Finn, who then got up and explained about his family.

"In public, I go under the name David Metz, but my name is Finn Kaspari. Yes, before you ask, I am of that Kaspari family, and I am somewhat aligned with my family's interests. I signed up for the Force to become an engineer, but I was too stubborn to take orders and I'm probably not suited to the Force, anyway. I wanted to be independent from my family. I have grown up in a world where my parents, my siblings, my cousins, my nieces and nephews are all involved in a business of some sort. I don't always agree with those businesses. You will know the many stories and the gossip that circulates about my family. I am not here to justify or excuse any of it. You can think what you want. I am interested in a business opportunity unrelated to my family, while at the same time attempting to fight corruption and other problems in the Federacy Assembly. Those things are not why I am here. In fact, I've gone through a rough stage and haven't been useful to anyone recently. Tina and her son were so kind to help me when I felt lonely and lost. My marriage had disintegrated and my family didn't want me, or so I thought. But the Kaspari blood is stronger than I thought. To be a Kaspari means being in business. It doesn't mean being famous or the subject of gossip. It doesn't really matter what my family thinks of me, not in this dangerous world. I want to make sure that influence and knowledge don't fall into the wrong hands. This is why I have stayed with Tina, why I have not misused any of my family's funds, which I don't currently have access to, but which I could ask for if I wanted. It is why I have remained quiet."

Next in line was Thor, who explained he had been a well-known engineer and had been forced to retire from the Force after his accident. He said that he had a lot of knowledge of different aircraft and other machines, and that he would be happy to help anyone who needed his service. The Freerangers didn't question how he would do this while he was blind.

Jens, Rex and Rasa said they had knowledge about security systems and would be happy to help, too.

Tina went on, "So this is the background. This is all a long-winded way of telling you what I want and how I think we can solve this situation. People inflicted with this genetic mutation are slowly taking over the institutions of the Federacy. We can't expect help from them. I propose to gather as many researchers as possible, and find out what we can about the infection, how to cure it or stop it. It's turning people into mindless monsters. Meanwhile, the war will rage on. Artan and his pirates will continue to attack stations of the Federacy, and the Federacy has enough people that it will continue to fight back. I suspect a lot of stations will continue to change hands from one to the other, and because of distances and lack of communication, the situation will be at least as chaotic as it is today. I need a safe place to do this research."

"That's all very well, but why us?" Clementine asked. "The Federacy doesn't care about us, they consider us criminals, they don't want to talk to us and we're not interested in them. Why should we be involved?"

"Because authorities don't care about you."

"They do care about us for as long as we deliver food."

"We understand your ships can still take us to the station."

"Wait, I thought you wanted to leave the system?"

"We do, but first we need to pick up people from Aurora Station. We also need some parts for the ship."

"How much do you pay?"

"We don't have much money."

"Ha, that's what they all say. What about that big military force that owns this ship?"

"The ship was captured and held by the pirates, and the Federacy is cautious about re-integrating it into the fleet."

She snorted. "So they're not talking to you."

From the corner of her eye, Tina spotted Yonta wanting to interrupt, but Aliz held up her hand to stop her.

Tina continued, "They are still talking to us, but they're not offering help. At any rate, I am not affiliated with the Federacy Force. This is *my* request, not an official Force proposal. I'm making it to you, because Finn spoke highly of you. The Federacy Force may have money, but they're not providing it. Money won't help us, anyway. Aurora Station is in pirate hands. We need a lift there to pick up our friends and some parts to make sure that the ship doesn't explode. We can barter things in return, within reason. I am sure we can negotiate about this."

A more interested look came over Clementine's face, shrewd almost. Tina remembered her interest in the ship. She would have to make sure that the Freerangers understood that the crew of the *Manila* were not defecting and the ship was not for sale. That was not the type of deal she wanted to do.

Tina added, "Our proposal would involve giving you a share in the outcome of our work."

She explained that when they found a way to stop or cure the infection, they would need a trade network to sell it to all human settlements and that the Freerangers could do that.

Clementine said, "We will need to look at this. With the war, our shipworlds need better technology, so maybe yes, we might be interested, if there is a possibility that our young people could learn."

"Definitely. Once we've established a research centre, we will need as many hands as possible."

"Hmmm."

Yes, she seemed definitely interested.

Tina continued, "Then let us talk about how to retrieve a couple of people from the civilian part of the station."

Clementine thought for a while.

"Will you pay extra for that?"

"I haven't discussed precise amounts because the payment we can offer is not defined by amounts—"

"What if our price for retrieving those people is to have some of our crew on this ship when this ship flies out of the system?"

Several women of the crew protested at the same time.

Tina looked at Aliz and knew that things would have to be pretty dire for her to give permission to take in Freeranger crew.

"I don't think the captain will agree to that."

But Clementine went on, "Those people you are going to retrieve from the station, are they people who know how to fly the ship or are they just going to add to the crew that needs to be looked after?"

This was a pointed question, and one that had been playing in the back of Tina's mind. Was there anyone at the station who could provide serious help for Aliz?

She met Clementine's eyes. "Does your group include people who could help fly the ship?"

"We can provide all kinds of people. You have seen how easily we board ships. Our clan includes people with a wide range of skills for a wide variety of ships. We also own every single simulation that was ever made."

"Simulations are no substitute for the real thing," Aliz said, her tone curt.

"I understand, but in absence of the real thing, they are better than nothing. If your new passengers are just civilians, you're going to bring a bunch of nothings on your ship."

No one could object to that.

Finn said, "I would be in favour."

Several of the crew gave him wide-eyed looks.

Clodine began, "But you know nothing—"

Clementine continued, "We know nothing about military ships? Do you really think that the military ships that the Federacy takes out of circulation get scrapped and quietly disappear? No, the military strips all the sensitive material out of them and sells them on. To us and other shipworlds. Several of our ships that we use for trading are ex-military ships. We know Federacy warships in and out."

"You own military ships? I don't believe that. You're just bluffing," Cally said.

But Aliz was quietly shaking her head. Tina herself had seen the ships being decommissioned and had always wondered what happened to them once they left active service. If these families bought those ships, they would be intimately familiar with all their operations, and, with ships past a certain age, of their failings. Of course, the *Manila* was not an old ship. Still, like the simulations, it was not a poor substitute.

She said, "Well, let's just talk about making a deal to get the scientists off the station and escape the system, and then when we're safe, we can negotiate."

"Hmmm," Clementine said. "If I agree, we may put our community at risk."

"I don't deny that."

"Besides payment or trades in the short term, why would we risk ourselves in the long term? We need to know more about the payoffs."

"I want to put up a research unit and need the space and safety to conduct our work. I'm offering for you to take part in selling the results, when there is something to be sold. If we find a compound that stops the infection, Finn here can help you make contacts to sell it. I cannot promise great riches, but I can promise that you won't lose money, and you might even be viewed as an important enough entity that the Federacy Assembly is forced to start listening to you, if you choose to go this way. I would leave that up to you. The only thing I am asking is that you help transport as many researchers as possible to a safe place."

"What do you call a safe place?"

"I don't know yet. A station or a city where we can do our work. We're likely to need help, so your people are welcome to help us with the research."

There was some silence after she finished speaking. Clementine and Rubiano looked at each other. Tina thought she spotted a small smile on Rubiano's face, but she couldn't be sure.

"We will have to talk about this with the rest of our family," Clementine said. "We will also consult the heads of the other families and the other shipworlds."

"You need their permission? I thought you were at war with each other?"

"That's another lie you people like to tell each other. That we're barbarians only capable of fighting. That's not us, but the foul people who have sullied our name. We used to take pride in being called pirates until those monsters arrived. After that, Federacy people started cutting our contracts and ignoring us, and then locking up some of our members. We have nothing to do with those disgusting creatures."

"Your know that Artan has his base on Aurora Station and that they're infecting more people there?"

"Yes." Clementine's voice was dark.

"The Federacy's approach has been to fight these people with weapons, but that's becoming very hard when new armies are created all the time, and when those armies include familiar people and loved ones that have been infected. Sending war ships is not a solution. We need to stop the spread of this infection with scientific means, by providing medicines, or a cure. That's what I'm asking you to help me do. And if we find something and we can sell it, you're welcome to share in the profits."

"Yes," Clementine said again. "We need to speak to the others. These are large and important decisions."

CHAPTER TWENTY-SIX

THE FREERANGERS RETURNED to their ship, leaving behind a tense silence. As soon as the group was gone, an argument broke out about whether the women should or shouldn't have trusted them.

Tina had enough and went to her cabin hoping to get some sleep. Rae wasn't there, and although Tina was still worried about her, she also didn't have the time or energy for long discussions, but she still felt guilty about being glad that she wasn't there.

Rae was an enigma in the same way Finn was difficult: paranoid, worried about strange things, and probably damaged by growing up in a world far removed from normal people's reality.

But she could use Rae.

Tina drifted off into a few blissful hours of sleep.

When she woke up, Rae still wasn't there, but a small light burned in the corner of the room, so she had probably been in.

Tina went back to the mess, where she found all the women of the crew there, gathered in a serious meeting. Had they even slept at all?

Evelle must have heard a noise at the door when Tina came in, and turned around.

"Oh, hi, Mum."

"Has anything happened?" Tina said. "Where are Finn and Rex and the others?"

"This is a matter for us crew only," Yonta said, her voice prim.

"We needed to discuss our way forward," Evelle explained.

Seriously, had they been discussing this all the time?

"Have you heard from the Freerangers?"

"Yes. They agree to help us," Aliz said.

"Isn't that good? I thought we all agreed on this being our only option."

"We did, but it's not as simple as that. This is a highly experimental ship that we have sworn to protect. Allowing outsiders to take control over operations of the ship would normally require many types of permissions and contracts. By allowing these people on board, we will break our oath."

"For a good reason. Without their help, none of the crew will survive and the ship will fall into the hands of enemies."

"That is only a mitigating factor at best. The Freerangers are not just any contractors. They are opportunists. They will try to get as much out of their dealings with us as they can. We need to make sure that we show them nothing the Federacy Force wouldn't want them to see, and we all need to be aware of what the procedures are."

"How can they help fly the ship if we don't show them anything?"

Evelle sighed and blew out a breath. "We want to have positions to go back to. Some of us have family in the Force. We may disagree with the Force's actions, but none of us can afford to be dishonourably discharged."

Several others nodded.

Really? "Would they dishonourably discharge you for trying to keep the ship in one piece and returning it to base?"

Dishonourable discharge was the domain of rare cases of flagrant rule-breaking and bribery.

No one answered that question. Tina looked from one to the other. Several women averted their eyes. Tina got a very bad feeling about this.

"This is not about letting the Freerangers into the ship, right? What actually happened when you were captured? Did one of the crew betray you?"

After another long silence, it was Lisette who replied. That was a surprise, because she tended to be quiet.

"They betrayed us."

Her voice was quiet.

"By 'they', you mean...?"

"Federacy Sector Command."

No one looked at Tina as Lisette said that.

She continued, "I was on duty and I overheard the Sector Command speaking to a third party just before we came out of the jump. I'm sure it was an accident that the communication was broadcast to us. I didn't understand what I heard until it was too late. We didn't become isolated from the fleet after an attack by pirates, as Aliz said earlier. We were abandoned and betrayed. The rest of our fleet had already joined the pirates before we exited the jump. Once we came out of the jump and found ourselves facing thousands of pirate ships, and the other ships in our fleet out of range, the captain understood we'd been set up. We fled, but we had little chance, because the other ships knew everything about our planned moves and their systems were still integrated with ours. The captain ordered all links to be severed, but that's hard to complete successfully when in the middle of a battle. So we had to capitulate—it was either that or be destroyed. Now we're on our own. It's a matter of time before the pirates come back to mop us up. There will be no fleet nearby to help us because they were never loyal to the Federacy, anyway."

Tina looked around the circle of faces and saw in the women's expressions that they all knew this was true.

"But why then do you still want to obey the upper command and follow your orders and protect the ship from strangers?"

"Because what we don't know is how much the Upper Command at Olympus knows about the betrayal, or whether they are betrayed, too. Worse than hanging around here forever would be to be chased by both the pirates and the Federacy, because we can't outrun the Federacy ships if they get it into their minds that we're traitors. They would make an example of us, or we'd disappear, never to be heard from again. All of us would like to go home one day. There are too many of us already not going home."

There were nods all around the group, and grim expressions on faces.

Tina said, "So the situation at the Federacy Assembly and Force headquarters is worse than you thought?"

"We don't know, and therefore, we want to be careful not to burn any bridges. If the Upper Command at Olympus wants us to take action against the Sector Command, which has joined the pirates, then we want them to know that we're still ready. We don't want them to think that we've gone rogue. We had this meeting to make sure that all of us understand this and we can move forward."

"That is how accepting help from the Freerangers fits into it?"

"Yes. It will be the crew's purpose to get to a safe place to have the ship fixed, to source reliable crew and then wait for orders to rejoin the Federacy Force command. We will accept the Freeranger's assistance as long as it benefits our recovery."

If ever Tina needed a reminder to be glad she'd left the

Force, this was it: all the ridiculous, kicking-in-open-doors bureaucracy.

To her, it was simple common sense to accept the help of anyone who offered it, and to trade off receiving help for money or favours. But no, apparently one needed an action plan.

Evelle continued, "Clementine says to prepare a small party of people to go across to the station. She says the family ship-world took delivery of some cargo that needs to go to the station, and they can take a few extras. They will send a ship that has a short distance passenger capacity of over a hundred if those people are happy to strap themselves in the cargo hold. It's up to us to get those passengers to the docks."

No more mention of going back for their mates, huh?

Well, one good thing had come out of the horrible events of the past day: it had really brought home Tina's point about the risk the three men posed to the ship.

Evelle continued, "So it's up to us to determine the best people to go. I suggest they will need to be people who are familiar with the station. None of us have ever been to this station, so I will leave deciding that to you."

"Thank you."

And Tina meant it. While she had been asleep, Evelle and Aliz had brought the other women in line in a way only career military would treat each other.

Tina made her way to the *Alethia* where she assumed the others would be.

And indeed, they were in the main cabin. Thor was making tea.

He always did this when people arrived at his place, or when he faced a question he couldn't answer, or a situation that required consideration. As if the very act of making tea calmed him down.

Tina accepted an anti-spill cup of hot tea and told them what the crew had decided.

Thor said, "Well, I'm glad they finally let go of this idea that they could rescue their crew mates. I've tried for years to make people understand that once someone falls under the influence of the pirates, it's almost always pointless trying to rescue them."

The implied horror is his statement made Tina shudder. Imagine seeing your friends and lover taken prisoner and knowing that the next tentacled monster you ran into could be one of those people.

Tina said that they could put together a small group to collect Arkady, Yalinda, Jette and any other scientists who would like to come.

Jens spoke up. "There is only one problem. We haven't heard from any of them since we escaped. I've sent them several messages."

That was a worry.

"What do you think could have happened?"

Thor replied. "I don't know. We've always been able to walk to each other's place. I never contacted any of them with messages."

"Have you checked whether they posted to the discussion boards?" Tina asked.

Jens said, "I did. None of them have said anything on those groups since we left the station."

"Can you reach them through the groups?"

"I tried." He shrugged. "Nothing."

Tina blew out a breath and looked at Finn. "What do you think? Do we take the risk?"

Thor said, "The Freeranger ship is going to the station anyway as far as I understand. These people can pretty much go wherever they want."

"That's because they've always pretended not to be interested in politics, just in selling things," Finn said.

"We should be on that ship. I feel obliged to do something. I failed Arkady's brother," Tina said. "I don't want to have it on my conscience that he's in trouble, I could have done something and didn't."

"But you're likely to need more than just a handful of people," Finn said.

"What is this you?" Tina said. "You're coming."

Finn shook his head. "I went into the station twice and got out twice. I was careful the first time, lucky the second. I am pretty sure that I won't get out the third time."

"Then who?"

"I will come," Rex said.

"No, you will not."

"Is this about my supposed formidability again?"

"You stand out far too much. They will know that we have you. There aren't that many people looking like a giant robot."

"Then you should've left me in my old harness."

Tina pulled a face. That would have been even worse.

Jens said in a soft voice, "I can come."

Tina looked at his skinny form and then pictured Freeranger robes on him and then realised that he was probably the perfect companion. He also knew a lot about the station's computer systems. She hated asking his father, but Thor nodded. "We've got to give it to the younger generation at some point. I wouldn't be any good because of my eyes."

So it was settled. Tina and Jens would go. Rex was disappointed, but she gave him the task of keeping in contact with Jens and trying to contact Arkady.

Tina asked when they were leaving, and Aliz told her that she wanted the Freeranger ship away from the *Manila* before she handed over to Evelle, so it would probably be soon.

Tina planned on using her third ID, retiring Louise Metvier, but didn't know if it would be necessary. Neither Clementine nor Aliz had said anything about this. Just that they would have access to the station.

But first, she and Jens would have to go to the Freeranger ship.

The Freerangers were going to use their boarding line again.

She received instructions from the family on how to use the pulley system. It was remarkably like the systems she'd used for EVA at Project Charon. In fact, knowing what she knew now about what happened to retired military ships, she suspected the two to be the same.

Jens, however, had only done the most basic of EVA training, the version children got at school, which included a session in a training room wearing vacuum suits, but never actually went outside.

His face was pale when she helped him close the helmet. She also realised that her earlier thought that he and Rex would have enough simulation experience to fly the Dragon fighters was ridiculous. There was so much more to being a fighter pilot than simply operating the equipment. Being aware of what to do in an emergency was one.

She put a hand on his arm. "Hey, I'll help you. We'll be tied to the line and I'll be right behind you."

He nodded, still not looking convinced.

Cally announced that the line from the Freeranger ship had attached to the outside of the hull.

With the line arrived a young man who helped them out the airlock.

The light from the system's sun reflected off the side of the Freeranger ship and cast the line in sharp shadow against the brilliant surface.

Tina clipped on the line and told Jens to relax, because he would be tied to the line and both ships with two separate mechanisms.

Tina was the first to step out of the ship, then Jens and then the Freeranger man.

The pulley transported them along the cable that stretched and jiggled as the ships drifted.

They moved out of the shadow of the *Manila* into the light. It grew hot inside the suit.

There were no mishaps this time.

From inside the bridge room, the distance between the ships might have seemed short, but out here it was quite far away. Tina was sweating in the suit. She looked over her shoulder several times to make sure that Jens was all right and still following, which he was.

In fact, after having gotten over the terrifying feeling of stepping into space, he seemed to quite enjoy it. Tina had to turn down the volume of the helmet loudspeaker with all his chatter about the things he could see on the outside of the *Manila*.

Tina was more concerned with the Freeranger ship, basking in blazing sunlight.

The only sign that this long, skinny structure belonged to the family were various signs painted in blue on the hull of the living compartment. An airlock door was open on the side. Tina made it to the hull and followed the trail of handholds that led to the airlock, noticing the strange construction of the outer surface, consisting of plates with rivets. It had been ages since people used those.

She wondered how old the ship was. A lot older than any of the military ships, she guessed.

She and the Freeranger man helped Jens into the airlock and as soon as they were in, the door shut.

The cubicle was cramped, and didn't appear to have a magnetic surface for their boots to stick to, only a couple of odd-looking handholds.

At least the hissing of air was familiar. Then the inner door opened, and Tina stepped into a world that she had never thought she would visit.

CHAPTER TWENTY-SEVEN

WHEN THE DOOR to the airlock opened, a waft of earthy-smelling air surrounded them. Tina had expected the usual bright lights and clean corridors, but it was rather dark inside the space beyond. Her eyes needed to get used to the low level of light before she could figure out what she was seeing.

The space in front of her was cavernous, cris-crossed by struts and bars that formed the internal support structures of the habitat. Cubicles the size of a tiny room hung off those bars. Because there was no gravity, they pointed in all directions.

Some of those cabins were completely closed, with a differently coloured light next to the entrance for each, others were partially open, and through the open sides she could see people. Men, women, families, children. All of those people watched her from within their little cabins that were decorated with soft furnishings and even plants. Cactuses.

Who said that a ship needed corridors and rooms and things like that?

Soft music played in the background.

"Welcome to the Shipworld Mara," a voice said.

Tina had to look around to see where the voice came from.

The figure she recognised as Clementine was floating through the hall, pulling herself along by the ship's support struts and the corners of the cabins.

Several other people had also gathered on the metal bars and at the entrance to the cabins. Other cabins were hastily swung around so that the open side faced Tina.

There were even more people inside.

What had Clementine said about there only being fifty people in this family? Tina didn't believe that for one moment.

"Look at all the children," Jens said. His voice was soft and hadn't yet broken like Rex's.

Clementine had come closer, her greying hair floating around her in a halo. A middle-aged man and a younger woman accompanied her.

"We have little time to get ready," she said. "You took long enough to get here."

"I'm sorry. Jens here was unused to EVA practice."

She gave him a sharp look. "What? Did your parents not teach you this?" Then she looked at Tina.

"He's not my son, and my son, who is at the ship, never learned this either. There was no need. He grew up at Cayelle."

"They're both in space now. That means there is a need." Her voice sounded rather prim. "How else can he work?"

"Jens here is still at school." Or he would be, if not for the pirates.

Jens cast nervous glances at the young man who helped them across. Without his helmet, he looked little older than Jens.

Tina let it rest. There was no time to explain the concept of minority, and to do so would be pointless, anyway. These people clearly lived in very close groups where no one worried about things like childhoods and child labour.

If they were going to spend more time with these people, that discussion would undoubtedly come up in the future.

Right now, they needed to get going.

"Thank you for being so kind to help us," Tina said. Although she wasn't so sure who was helping whom. She understood that the family had planned to return to the station, anyway.

They looked so comfortable, so totally in control. So different from the situation aboard the *Manila*.

Clementine said, "First we have to get you into suitable attire. Have you been in contact with your people at the station?"

"No, we haven't, so our part of the expedition maybe quite short."

Tina preferred not to think about what she would do if she couldn't find Arkady or any of the other scientists.

How she would explain it to Thor.

What it would mean for her plans.

Thor would be devastated to know that even more of his friends had fallen into pirate hands. She would have to source people from elsewhere.

Clementine said, "Remember that people from the ship-worlds don't normally venture far into the stations. We don't like stations and we don't know too many people who live there permanently. We come to the docks, we may come to the commercial offices and to the Ship Supply Office. That is about it."

"I have another disguise for going into the station," Tina said.

She showed them her station overalls. Clementine approved.

"Well then, you better go. We mustn't miss our docking window."

She showed Tina into a room where the middle-aged man gave her a blue robe. It was a heavy-duty garment, laced with unfamiliar smells that were, to be honest, disturbingly chemical and less natural than she would have expected. Tina donned the robe over her clothes. It floated in the air around her. A young woman then helped her with the elastic bands that held the fabric in place around her upper arms, lower arms, upper legs and lower legs. A belt did the job around her waist.

Jens was also getting this treatment, and when she looked at him, wearing a robe, with the bands around the arms and legs to make the robe stay in place, with his hair tied up, he looked just like a Freeranger. She suspected that she herself would make a much less convincing picture.

Her hair was too short for one. She was also not lanky enough. She'd grown up on a planet, and everything about her stature said that.

Then they were ready, packed up all their clothes, got a set of emergency evacuation suits to take to the shuttle in case they were needed, and followed the middle-aged man and a young woman to another part of the ship.

The area of the ship they traversed also consisted of open spaces with those same small cabins which could be moved around and used as required. Sometimes they were for people to live in—and she spotted ones that housed bunches of teenage friends—and sometimes they were for storing cargo.

Did they ever turn on the rotating habitat? She asked their companions. The woman said that the rotating habitat hadn't been operational for as long as she had been alive.

In civilian ships, the artificial gravity functioned to keep the crew healthy. Federacy Force ships didn't always use it, because the rotating habitat took away the ability of a ship to manoeuvre quickly, and limited the amount of engine power. But this meant that the crew had to spend a lot of time in the gym, which was all right, because there wasn't usually a lot to do during long journeys, anyway.

But how would these people combat the effects of weight-lessness? They all seemed to be quite healthy.

Via an open passage, they came to a docking bay, with entrances to docked shuttles on several levels.

Just six people were going in the shuttle. Apart from the middle-aged man and young woman they had already met, there were two younger men already on board.

The crew introduced themselves, but they spoke in such an unfamiliar dialect that Tina couldn't make out what their names were. Nor did she catch what the ship was going to deliver. It seemed rude and unimportant to ask them to repeat.

The middle-aged man said, "When you arrive at the station, we will give you a time for departure. You have to make this time, because we can't wait for you. If you're not there, and you get left behind, that means the pilot will be in trouble. Avoid that."

Tina nodded. She looked at Jens, but in the past few hours she had already asked him so often whether he had heard from Arkady that she was sure he would say something if he had.

The mission was risky and stupid. For her safety, and that of others, she should call it off and accept that Arkady was in trouble and could not contact anyone. But that would feel like abandoning him to his fate, like she had done with all her colleagues. That was unacceptable.

None of the other researchers from Project Charon who had raised concerns about the project had fared too well. Tina had to do her best for Dimitri's memory.

She had to try, even if only because she needed the scientists.

The shuttle was another item from times past. It felt flimsy, like a couple of boxes put together, designed for carrying cargo and not for comfort. The crew stations were at the back of the cabin, and from her position Tina could see the navigation screen and visuals of the station. Not that the screens displayed very much. The *Alethia* was twenty-five years old, but its external visuals were so much better. Did people really still navigate by sight?

The pilot took his position at the controls. The rest of the crew were all already strapped in.

Like so many of the things, the crew stations could swivel according to where the gravity was coming from. Tina released the lever that held the seat in position, but her seat swung around so that she was looking at Jens upside down.

He was laughing.

"Not used to weightlessness?" said the young woman, while she took up her seat on Tina's other side. She gave Tina's leg a push so that she swivelled back the way she and Jens were facing. "Here, lock the seat with this lever."

"I just undid it because I assumed that we're going to take the gravity direction from the station."

"We will—when we've arrived."

Tina resisted making further remarks. In *some* ships, like the *Alethia* the seats held springs that stopped them swivelling around at the slightest movement.

The shuttle detached from the main ship. A brief burst of the engine made the distance bigger. The huge shape of the *Manila* came into view, back-lit by the glow from the nearby star.

Then they retreated further, revealing additional specks that were too bright to be floating asteroids.

"Are those commercial ships?" Tina asked.

"They belong to shipworld Mara," the young woman said.

"Are they all in this area?"

"Loosely, yes. We always stay together so we can back each other up. This is the big mistake that many fleet captains make. Three or four ships do not make a fleet. If something happens to one ship, the entire mission has to be abandoned. Our mission is survival, and prosperity of our next generation. We never lose sight of that."

And non-shipworld people, apparently, lost sight of the next generation. Really? She wondered why else she would spend fifteen years building a safe place for her son. Tina was getting rather tired of the self-righteousness of these people.

Then again, she might be the same if she lived in an isolated environment like this.

The trip to the station was only short and nothing much else was said on board, except for the pilot speaking to the station. It was not busy at the docks, that much Tina could see from her position, so the docking procedure was quick. There were none of those annoying checks that the *Alethia* had been subjected to when coming to the station, because these Freeranger people were known to the station authorities, and because they were bringing items that the station needed.

With a small thump, they had returned to Aurora Station. The station's gravity kicked in. Tina swivelled her seat around. It was time to go.

CHAPTER TWENTY-EIGHT

JENS WAS GETTING ready to leave the shuttle, with all his devices in his pockets. He looked convincingly like a Freeranger. Tina only hoped that she passed as well.

She checked all her false identification cards, that they were all tucked away in different pockets in her clothes. She checked the pockets and checked them again.

The door opened, letting in a waft of unpleasant smelling, humid air.

Jens frowned. "Does this place always stink like this?"

Tina barely remembered last time when the *Alethia* docked at the station. It seemed so long ago. She vaguely remembered thinking that there was a stale smell, but didn't remember whether it had been this bad. She didn't think so.

A man in station overalls came to the opening. He said something in Sinolese that Tina didn't understand, but the Freeranger crew understood and acknowledged. She and Jens walked past him with a young man from the crew who was arranging the delivery of the cargo.

Jens only spoke when they were away from the ship.

"Did you hear that? He was telling us specifically not to go into the station."

"No. I don't speak Sinolese terribly well. Did he say why?"

"He didn't. He said to stay in the restricted area."

"But we can reasonably be expected to visit the Ship Supply Office?"

"I don't know. He didn't say."

They followed the signs that pointed to the Ship Supply Office, and then suddenly they were in front of it, and it was not the same place where it had been the last time. Well, what the... Station authorities had set up a new temporary office on this side of the checkpoint. Well, shit.

Jens said, "They really don't want us to go into the station."

"I wonder why."

"I hope my friends are all right." His eyes were wide.

They still had to put in their order for supplies, and it was busy in the office with the usual crowd of merchant pilots, family members of pilots and other lackeys.

"I can wait here while you go," Jens said.

Tina looked around, a feeling of despair coming over her. It had taken her so long to make this decision to come back for Arkady, and now she couldn't see him. It might already be too late to save him and the other scientists.

But she couldn't just barge into the station. She needed to know more.

She spoke to a few people who were waiting in the long lines. She said that she had come here hoping to visit a friend on the station, and that she didn't know how to get there.

Several people frowned at her Freeranger robe. A few people obviously weren't buying her disguise. No, Freerangers didn't visit people in the stations, because they knew no one there. Or they made a point of not knowing anyone there, or made a point of pretending they didn't.

Or something. Her disguise wasn't very convincing, and she knew it.

"It's impossible to go into the station," a man told her. "There are checkpoints set up everywhere. The pirates are shipping the entire civilian population out. This station is going to be the pirates' base, apparently. All those people were told to leave their homes and come to the docks to await a flight elsewhere. They must all be waiting around here."

"Where are they being taken?"

He shrugged. "I don't know. Some pirate world, I guess."

Tina returned to Jens and asked if he could still access those programs that allowed him to see where people were in the station.

He did, but the latest scan he could access was a few days old, taken just after he and his father had left the station. It did, however, show a concentration of people in the docks area.

"This man told me the pirates are telling the population to leave. When you last left the station, was there any sign of this?"

"No, but I was asleep when we left, and my father always organised everything so that if it was necessary, we could just pick up our bags and walk out. A lot of the things in the apartment had their dedicated places, and there were a couple of containers that were important, and the rest we would just leave behind. He was always talking about that since I was little. So he woke me up when he was ready and we left, just like he said we would. I was very happy that we were going to join you."

But clearly, leaving the place where he had grown up, and his friends, had shaken him more than he wanted to admit.

"How come your dad suspected something like this?"

"I don't think he did. He says to always be prepared because that was what they did in the Force. He's just always scared and doesn't trust people much."

"He trusted us."

"Certain types of people."

"But did you see signs the pirates were moving people off the station when you left?"

He shook his head.

Although there had been signs that people were being moved even when she was at the station. Those people had been just prisoners, not the civilians.

She sighed.

"Well, all of this doesn't help us much if we can't get out of this area. We don't have much time."

Jens met her eyes. "You think we should try to reach them?"

"That's why we're here." Of course, now she regretted having taken only one other person. Even if she'd had Rex, it would have been much easier to break through any barriers. Never mind that Rex would have made an even less convincing Freeranger than she, and there would have been a risk that he wouldn't have been allowed in the station at all.

She pressed her arm against her body. The hard shape of the Fireseed cut into her side. She might need to use it this time.

She made a decision. "Let's go."

They'd put in the ship supply order electronically. It may or may not be delivered in time, but Clementine had said that this load of supplies wasn't vitally important. The shipworlds always took in supplies when the opportunity arose, which made that their ships were well-stocked and could go without.

She and Jens left the temporary office and navigated through the passages to a point where they couldn't go any further.

A couple of pirate guards stood at a temporary barrier behind which there was a stretch of empty corridor, followed by another barrier with more guards.

The sound of many voices, talking, yelling, drifted from the space beyond.

Tina and Jens retreated before the guards had noticed them.

"What's going on there?" Tina asked, not expecting an answer.

Jens was looking at his screen again.

"There is a passage," he said. "It goes right along here and here and with a bit of luck you can come out in this corridor, which looks like it's on the other side of this checkpoint. I can hack into the access panel. We can pretend that we're maintenance personnel."

"You're on," Tina said.

She looked over his shoulder at the map of the nearby area. There was indeed a small chamber that led from an area in the docks over the top of the passages to another area, where there was an air compression plant or something similar.

The passage led over the top of the area where they had seen the new checkpoint.

They looked around for a public amenities area that was not too busy and got changed out of the Freeranger robes into their overalls.

Jens had gone back to being a teenage boy when he came out. This disguise didn't suit him half as well as the Freeranger robe. He looked too young. He'd have to be her apprentice.

He had stuffed the Freeranger robe into his bag, but a part was still sticking out. She tucked it back and did up the fastening for him.

He frowned at her.

Yes, that was right, he had grown up without a mother who would have fussed over details of his clothing. His father would have been unable to see.

Tina strapped on the tool belt and gave him a couple of tools.

Then they went back to the checkpoint.

The access panel was just around the corner, fortunately out of view of the guards. Jens had no trouble opening it, and he crawled in.

He said, his voice muffled, "It's very tight in here, but there is a ladder. I'm going to climb up a bit so that you can come in, but then you have to close the door. Make a light, because it will get very dark and crowded with both of us in here."

Tina entered when his feet disappeared up the ladder. It was indeed very cozy inside.

When she pulled the door shut, they were enclosed in full darkness.

She turned on the little light on the shoulder of the station overalls, and they climbed up. They came out in a space where fat tubes ran along the top of the passage below. Air rushed through some of the tubes, evidenced by the moving needles on the flow meters. Other pipes contained water. They had to crawl underneath the biggest pipes, and step over others to get to a narrow aisle lined with control panels. The air compressor made a lot of noise. They walked along the passage for a short distance, and then Jens lifted a grate in the walkway. A narrow ladder led into a dark hole. Jens climbed down, and Tina followed him.

She could hear the sound of many voices before they reached the bottom. Angry voices, shouting voices, the sounds of scuffles and fights.

"What's going on in there?" Jens said.

But Tina didn't know that either. It did not sound good.

CHAPTER TWENTY-NINE

JENS CAREFULLY PUSHED OPEN the access panel. Standing behind him, still on the ladder, Tina had a view through the opening of the legs and shoes of many people shuffling along the corridor, all in the same direction. The sound of shouting became stronger, but now that Jens had opened the panel, it sounded like it came from slightly further down the passage.

"It's very busy out there," Jens said, peeking through the gap.

"Any pirates?"

"Not that I can see."

"Then let's go."

First Jens and then Tina crawled out of the access panel.

Several people gave them strange looks.

The crowd formed a long and disorderly queue waiting for something at the end of the passage, likely to get through a checkpoint.

A couple of armed guards stopped the line at the end. Some people a few rows back from the guards yelled, but the guards didn't react and it was impossible to hear what they said.

For now, the situation seemed reasonably under control.

Jens pushed the panel shut and keyed the lock to a code he generated on his pad. Nothing could keep this young man out of anything.

Tina and Jens made their way through the passage, away from the checkpoint. The people here we are all normal station residents. Tina listened for comments about where they were all going, or why they waited here. The crowd waited calmly. A bit impatient, yes, but without signs of panic.

The crowd showed no signs of thinning out by the time Tina and Jens reached the turnoff to the part of the station where Jens and Thor had lived. Somebody had closed the passage with another temporary barrier, and two pirate guards stood on either side.

Well, crap.

Now what?

"There is another way," Jens said, without stopping.

Tina followed him. It got increasingly busy here, and the awkward toolkit she carried kept bumping into people.

But the second passage was closed off with a grate, too.

"It looks like they've closed all the apartments around here." Jens' face held a haunted expression. He'd lived here. His friends lived here.

Well, damn it.

As they stopped on the other side of the passage, looking in between the passing crowd through the grate, a group of people came out of a side passage into the deserted corridor on the other side of the barrier, and turned left, deeper into the closed area.

The person in front was a pirate, and the people following him were half transformed mutants, men all. Many only wore trousers, but no shirt. Their skin was grey and mottled. They walked silently, with powerful steps, their shoulders hunched.

What was the bet that these were new additions to the pirate force?

"They're taking up all of your old apartments for new troops," Tina said.

"This is where a friend of mine lives," Jens said. He looked horrified. "I wonder where he is."

The answer seemed obvious: in that mass of people that was trying to get away from the station. That's where Arkady would be.

She checked the time.

They didn't have long to check all these crowds of all these people, and they had no means of communication.

Tina felt the hope that they would rescue Arkady fall away from her. This was a ridiculous venture, but they had to try for as long as possible. Even if they could find only one person, that was one person saved.

Jens made the suggestion that if he put a BCD on the top of the fully extended arm of his probing tool, he could hold it over the heads of the crowd and scan it that way.

Tina had a much better idea. The arm was too flimsy to carry the weight of the screen, but she still had the security camera from the prison in her pocket. She pulled it out.

"Here, use that."

Jens laughed.

"You know, I can see how Rex is your son. You just give him mischievous ideas."

"I can assure you that he gets plenty of mischievous ideas by himself."

They fixed the camera on top of the extended arm with a bit of tape, connected the camera to a larger screen which Jens held at the bottom of the stick. Turning around offered them a view over the heads of the crowd, but they couldn't move the camera very fast, because there was a slight lag in the image appearing on the screen.

It was so busy in certain parts of the corridor that they couldn't get close enough to see people's faces. Tina despaired of all the people they missed, and all the people where they only saw the backs of their heads and had no hope of identifying. She was hoping that Arkady was with his friends and that at least one of them would turn around so that their face came into view. Also, Jette was quite tall, and her blond hair would stand out.

They kept an eye on the clock. Time was ticking away mercilessly. They didn't make half as much progress as they wanted, because whenever they spotted a guard, they had to back away and lower the camera.

There were so many people lined up everywhere.

The population of Aurora Station had been a million before the pirate trouble started. No one had published any figures since then. Rumours said that the population had declined a lot, but Tina saw little evidence for that.

Because there didn't seem to be much movement in the waiting crowds, guards made an effort to keep a path free where the mass of people blocked a thoroughfare.

Occasionally, bystanders asked Tina what they were doing, and Tina told them the truth, that they were looking for someone.

They received some strange comments, and other people said it was a good idea, and still other people told them that they had been separated from their family as well and could Jens and Tina help look for them, too. They acquired a few hangers-on who were desperate to find their loved ones.

It was getting close to the time where they would have to return to the ship, when Jens suddenly said, "There."

Tina's heart jumped. He held up the screen for her to look over his shoulder, and she saw them too. Arkady's grey hair, Jette with blonde hair, and Yalinda as well. With them were a couple of other people Tina recognised from the meeting in

Arkady's apartment, a handful of children, and a number of people who they didn't know.

Jens took the camera off the pole and tucked the screen away.

"Let's go and get them."

Now Tina wished she had brought Rex. It was so busy in the passage that it was hard to get through. She and Jens had to worm through the crowd, asking for people to get out of the way because they were maintenance personnel. But pretending to be a service technician only went so far. People turned around and made annoyed comments that everyone was waiting and no one would be allowed to jump the queue.

They couldn't call out to Arkady either, and they couldn't do anything else to catch their attention.

Jens was the smallest, and he didn't carry so many tools, so he pushed ahead and reached Arkady first. Tina was close enough to hear him say, "Hey Mister, did you want me to fix your ship?"

Arkady turned around. His eyes widened.

But unfortunately, at the word ship, a lot of people had turned around. Hope came to their faces. Ship? Was there someone who had a ship? Someone who could help them flee this station? She reached Arkady as well. Yalinda and Jette were with him, as well as some other people, including two men and two young girls, who looked like they were Yalinda's.

"We would like to discuss the maintenance of your craft," Tina said, her voice slightly raised. "It may be a few days before we can get the parts, but if you're okay with it, we might be able to fix it."

She was hoping that whatever these people were waiting for, it would happen sooner than a few days.

She made a movement with her head, indicating for Arkady and his companions to come with her.

He said something to Yalinda, and then he said to Tina in a soft voice, "How many can you take?"

"A decent group, probably about a hundred. I want you to gather all the scientists. This is not an easy ride off the station to somewhere you can catch other flights. It's quite unconventional, dangerous, and people who come with us are there for the long haul. I need scientists to work with me."

Arkady asked, "Do I have any time to get additional people?"

"Not really, not until we're in a safer place. It has taken us long enough to find you. I was just going to walk up to your apartment and collect you. I'm not sure what's going on here."

"We are being told to evacuate," he said. "The habitat is unstable. The pirates might be good at fighting, but they're not very good at maintaining things."

Tina hadn't even seen that much evidence that the pirates were terribly good at fighting either. There were just a lot of them at the station.

"We probably only have time to get just yourself and anyone who is around here. We need to get out as quickly as possible, because if we miss the departure window, we will all be stuck here with you."

Stations were dangerous places, where you had to come to get supplies, but where you were also likely to get into trouble.

Arkady nodded, spoke to Yalinda again, and she glanced at the man next to her. He was quite tall and thin, typical of a person who had grown up in space. He had dark skin, short-cropped hair and a short beard. "This is my husband, Benjamin. He is also a researcher."

Tina looked at the girls, both of them meeting her gaze with dark doe-eyes. The poor things had to be terrified in this forest of adults. "Those are your children?"

"Yes, they are. They're too young to be scientists."

"Don't worry, we will make scientists out of them."

A couple of other people also appeared to have joined the group. There was an older couple, two younger women, another family with three children, one of them a baby.

"These are our friends. They also work in research," Arkady said.

"Ready? Let's go then."

This time, Tina was at the front of the group.

Many people in the passage made annoyed comments about them going against the flow, but soon, the rumours came out that this group must have found a way off the station and that they knew how to circumvent the checkpoints. The tail of the group grew and grew. Soon, the group was so big that they could no longer move unnoticed. What was worse, there wasn't going to be enough room on the Freeranger shuttle for all these people.

"I think we're in trouble," Tina said.

"I might be able to do something," Jens said.

He had taken out his pad and was fiddling with something.

He said to Tina in a low voice, "I want everyone in our group to hold on to each other, and to look ahead to make sure we know which direction to take."

Tina relayed this message to Arkady, and he told Yalinda and her family behind him, and she told Jette.

Then Tina tried to orient herself. Jens was probably going to turn off the lights to create confusion. They didn't need to go far, just around the corner back to the other corridor, and then they needed to get past the checkpoint.

"Ready?"

Tina nodded that she was.

Jens was doing something on the screen. As she had predicted, the power in the corridor went out. They were plunged in total darkness.

All around them, people started screaming.

"Go forward," Jens said, and Tina pushed ahead, pulling

with her the human chain of people who held onto each other. When there were sounds that they people might not be able to hang on, she took the rope from her belt, passed it around to make sure everyone was tied up.

The emergency lighting came on, and the voice of a guard bellowed over the crowd, yelling for people not to panic.

That was easier said than done, especially for the untrained civilians, who had children and elders in their care.

In the chaos, Tina and her group managed to make it around the corner.

Now they faced a different problem. Armed guards.

And finally, it was coming to that stage where Tina would have to prove that she was ever part of the Federacy Force, had weapons training and knew how to create a chaos without getting anyone killed.

She pulled out the trusted Fireseed from her jacket. She contemplated where to aim to create the most panic and disruption.

She decided the control module of the checkpoint was probably it. If she was lucky, the thing might even explode. It would definitely fry the electronics.

She lifted the Fireseed, but it was hard to get a clear shot. There were too many people in this passage. Jens pointed to a power box on the side. She stepped on top of it.

Several people yelled out when they saw her gun. Time to ditch her disguise. It was now or never.

She took aim and pressed the release.

CHAPTER THIRTY

THE CHARGE HIT the screen of the closest console at the checkpoint. Those screens tended to be made from artificial glass, and warnings always circulated about how this material would explode into a shower of tiny pieces with huge temperature changes.

The glass did just that, exploding into thousands of fragments lit up like a fire cracker.

The heat started a fire inside the exposed panel of the machine.

People screamed and tried to push away from the black smoke.

Guards shouted for everyone to keep calm. A couple of emergency lights came on. Their yellowish light gilded the heads of the crowd, people moving and pushing, lifting children out of the crush.

Tina stood next to Jens on the box. The light lit up Arkady's greying hair and the tall form of Jette also stood out. The others gathered around them, bunched together. A couple of men had turned their backs to the crowd to protect the younger children. For a while, it was simply impossible to move.

But then space opened up. The checkpoint was down, and people streamed past the guards who could no longer control them, into the docks area of the station.

Where all these people were going was a big question. There were unlikely to be many ships available, and this would be the reason why the public was kept out of this area in the first place.

Tina and Jens would need to act quickly. If they were going to move with this large group, people would follow them, because people were desperate. The Freerangers were unlikely to have experience fending off large, desperate crowds.

She jumped off the box.

"Come on, follow me," she shouted.

Tina set off in the direction of the checkpoint. The scientists followed her. Many in the group still held hands, and they made sure that the children could pass safely. The surge forward of their group pushed other people aside.

Some people were already joining them. The group had gotten so much bigger.

The barriers at the checkpoint were abandoned, with the guards standing to the side. They had emptied a canister of foam to put out the fire in the console, but remained helpless against the surging tide of people.

But there was a hold-up further down. A barrier blocked the passage, consisting of a grate made from metal bars slotted into recesses into the walls.

People surged against the grate, which was not intended to withstand this amount of force. It moved, bulging ominously.

A man shouted, coordinating a lot of people to push together at the same time.

The slots holding the barrier in place broke with a snap on one side of the corridor. Sections of the wall cladding came out. The grate toppled outwards. People fell forward, and the crowd behind them surged through. A couple of guards on the other side watched with wide eyes and hands on their batons, but they did nothing.

Tina and her group followed. Jens was checking the map.

At the end of the corridor, the crowd turned left, while Jens told Tina the Freeranger ship was moored in the passage to the right. Because they were such a large group, a number of other people followed. Clementine had said the shuttle could take about a hundred, but it looked like they might have to accept a few more.

There was enough room inside the *Manila*, but it remained to be seen whether they had enough provisions for a long trip. They would make do. The Freerangers might have a solution. It would probably cost. Tina didn't think that these refugees from the station cared about money anymore. The group had acquired several families with young children. Did Freerangers recruit new members? Tina had no idea.

This passage was fairly quiet, but when they came to a t-intersection, it grew busy.

Pirate guards lined the walls, holding back the civilian crowd. Several of them looked alarmed, as if they were surprised by the sudden appearance of masses of people.

A bunch of pirates waited at the door to the lift.

Oh, damn, the pirates were bringing in another batch of prisoners. A hand of fear clamped around Tina's heart. What if the pirates had re-captured the *Manila* while she had been away? Both her children were aboard the ship. She had assumed that they were safe, but...

The lift door opened.

It contained not a group of prisoners, but a dignitary of some kind, a man in a spiffy red and navy outfit with shiny buttons and decorations. All around the walls of the lift stood a *lot* of pirate guards.

They ran out of the lift as soon as the door opened, clearing the way for their master. Not Artan, but a very human man, with brown hair and a short beard.

Tina realised too late that they were coming in her direction. Not just that, but the guards in the passage blocked her escape. They had pushed away all the others in her group so that she stood alone, surrounded by armed guards, facing the man in the fancy outfit.

Only then did she look into his face and recognised him: his brown eyes, his short beard, his very human, very normal face. A familiar face.

And a wave of hatred surged through her.

"Dexter."

He laughed. "You thought I was dead, right?"

It all came back to her: his ignoring of her warnings, his arrogance, his unfailing conviction that only he could be right. That smug expression on his face. That haughty tone in his voice.

"I'd assumed you had turned into a tentacled monster." She put as much hate in her voice as possible.

"I have something better than that. You can be part of it."

He turned sideways, as if observing himself in a mirror. Tina had to admit, he did look very muscled and healthy. His hair was lush and his short beard less grey than she remembered. She remembered the bumpy feeling of the scar on his forehead from a mishap in training. That scar was gone.

But she could see no sign of transformation into a mutant in him. His skin was smooth and pink, not grey.

"I don't care about anything you have to offer." Whatever story he would tell to make her feel sympathy for him, it was clear to Tina that he was not only a traitor, he was a coward, not having undergone the transformation into a pirate himself. What did he fear? Losing his precious mind?

"You do care, oh, you do. I can help you with many things.

Don't tell me that you wouldn't want to fix that precious son of yours."

"Son of *ours*. There is nothing wrong with him."

"You don't want him to be a normal boy? If I were you, I'd be ashamed that I'd allow him to walk around like some kind of degenerate cyborg. We could grow natural limbs for him. For yourself, wouldn't you want to erase the effects of age? Don't tell me you're as fit as you used to be, or look as good as you used to."

What the hell was that supposed to mean?

"Look, Dexter, we're finished. I'm not interested in what you have to say. Tell your lackeys to step back and we'll get out of the way."

He laughed again.

"Gullible, weak and naïve. I always knew you were those things. I didn't think you were dumb until now."

"We've had this discussion before, in different forms. You're telling me how wonderful your research is, never mind this stuff you tout as wonder medicine is dangerous? I'm not interested in talking to you."

"No, I think you're right. You're too far down the self-righteous path, but tell me, why are you shielding your son from me? If you insist that he is *my* son, why won't you let me talk to him? I'm sure he won't be as dismissive of the chance to be given proper limbs."

"Dexter, get your thugs out of my way."

"I'll let you go, but in return, I want to talk to the boy. That is my offer. I'll let you and your sorry band of misfits go. I'll even let you depart the system with that crippled ship. We obtained all we want from it, anyway. In return, I demand to talk to my son."

"After fifteen years of pretending he doesn't exist? No. You had your chance."

"How about I ask him?"

"He's not here."

"I am aware of that, but I know where to find him."

He came a step closer.

"You can try to run, but we know where you are."

And another step.

"We know where you've been."

Another step.

"We know your moves so well, we can even predict where you're going before you know it yourself."

"Dexter, you're an arsehole."

He laughed.

"You're welcome. You've said that before. I'm a very wealthy, healthy arsehole."

He took another step towards her.

"You can be a poor, unhealthy, sanctimonious speck of dust. I don't care. You'll die out in your pathetic corner of the galaxy. I don't care. Go. Take your band of losers and get out of here. Just let me talk to my son."

He had come close enough that she could feel his warmth and see every pore in his skin. Tina had no idea why she had ever loved this man. He'd been a manipulative bastard right from the beginning. He made deals. Give me this and you can have that. Never mind that the things he gave were not his to give or were hers to start off with.

She hated him.

She remembered the relief she felt when, at Cayelle, months passed without news from him. And she remembered how she decided she'd stop asking him for money for Rex's upbringing. Because she didn't want Dexter involved with Rex.

She gestured to Jens.

"Come. We're leaving. I have nothing more to discuss with this man."

During a few heart-stopping moments, no one moved.

Tina realised, too late, that Dexter might think Jens was his son.

Dexter met Jens' eyes. They were light blue-grey. Dexter's eyes were brown.

He looked at Jens' overalls. Dexter's eyebrows knitted together. He grabbed the fabric of Jens' overalls and pushed up the sleeve, revealing Jens' skinny arm. Not a metal arm.

"Hey! What are you doing?" Jens' eyes were wide. But he yanked the overalls out of Dexter's grip.

Dexter snorted. "Fuck off with your pathetic band of sorry losers and she-boys."

In one step, Tina had pushed Jens aside, lunged forward and hit Dexter smack on the cheek. The slap echoed in the passage.

Dexter grabbed her wrist like lightning. His hand was like a vice.

"What was that?" His voice was like a hiss.

"That was for treating me like your personal servant all those years."

She glared into his eyes. His cheek was going red. The inside of her hand burned with the intensity of the slap.

She wrenched her arm out of his grip, grabbed Jens by the shoulder and pushed him past Dexter and his astonished pirate guards to Arkady, Jette, Yalinda, their families and all the hangers-on.

"Come. Our flight is waiting."

Dexter's voice came down the passage. "Don't think for one moment that I will foget this. We will meet again, and I will speak to the boy. I know where to find you."

CHAPTER THIRTY-ONE

TINA WAS SEETHING.

It had been a long time since she had felt the burning anger that used to consume her in the days of her marriage to Dexter. It was not a good memory.

What did he think he was?

But she couldn't dwell on it. First, they had to get out of here.

The docks area was in chaos. They came past places where station employees were trying to stop people entering ships that were closed, past families begging anyone who looked like a merchant for passage off the station, people trying to barter their valuables for a ticket. People overwhelming ticket counters, people holing up a flight crew officer in a corner. One guard who came out of a slide passage was washed away by the stream of people.

The place had descended into chaos.

Tina worried their group would be too big to fit into the shuttle. The group behind her had grown in size even while walking through the docks.

They arrived at the entrance to the ship. The young Freeranger who stood guard looked at the group of people coming towards him, and his eyes widened.

Would they be able to take everyone?

Tina turned around at the entrance to the ship and faced the people behind her. She raised her voice.

"For those following along and who are not part of our group of scientists, you'll have to understand that we are not going to any of the stations where you can buy passage to other places or meet up with any of your relatives."

She positioned herself in front of the door to the craft, even while people still pushed from behind. People yelled behind them to stop pushing.

"We are going to a secret place, I don't even know where at this stage, where we will hide, for as much as several years, and we will try to find a treatment to the infection that inflicts the pirates and that is creeping into the rest of society. We won't come back to normal society until we have that solution, and then we will present it to the Assembly. We are not going to any of the other stations. You cannot get a lift with us to anywhere, and once you come with us, we cannot allow you to leave. Before I let you on board this ship, I ask for your absolute commitment, that you understand what I just said, because otherwise I will turn you around, because we cannot use people who are going to create trouble for us. Do you understand?"

The first people behind her were Arkady and his group, and they knew about this. She let them into the ship. The people behind them were also part of Yalinda's lab group, and they went in as well, but gradually, they came into people of the general population, and some people elected not to come, because they had thought that this was a way to get off the station.

"I'm sorry. Go to one of the regular shuttles if you just want a lift to another station or to another place where you can meet up with your relatives."

More people turned away, but in the end, quite a sizeable group of people remained, many of whom had never worked in research before. Some of them said they didn't mind giving it a try, and they had nothing else to do, anyway.

Some said that they had no families anyway, and Tina was wondering if some of those were of the group of homeless and whether Rasa might know any of them. And she might be taking on board a bunch of trouble.

But there was no time to worry about that. She consulted with the Freeranger crew about how many they could carry.

When she was about to close the door, a woman in the company of two burly guards came to the ship.

Tina recognised her.

It was the director of Aurora Station, Zia Partlow, Finn's ex.

"We don't offer lifts off the station," Tina said, and she went through her spiel again, by now well rehearsed.

Zia flicked her hand in the middle of it. "I don't care about any of this, but please hurry, because these miscreants have chased me out of my office and threatened to kill me. I have no doubt they'll do it if they find me here."

"Before I let you in, I have to ask this: do you understand we won't be going anywhere near places of authority, and that you won't be able to get a lift off the ship or out of the location where we are going for potentially several years?"

"Frankly, I don't care."

Her voice sounded ragged, and it was now that Tina noticed the dishevelled state of the two guards. One guard sported a rip in his uniform, the other appeared to have lost his belt, and his trousers hung perilously close to dropping to the floor. He also hadn't done up his shoes.

"What's going on in the station?" she asked.

"It's chaos. These criminals are turning it in to a war head-quarters. This utter rich boy dickhead has taken possession of *my* office and *my* staff. I put up with all of Artan's bullshit for the sake of keeping the population safe, because we had no other option, but I'm done. I'm finished."

Dexter, taking command of the station for the pirates.

"Do you understand that if we take you, you might not be able to report to your authorities?" Tina repeated the question.

"What are authorities worth if they won't help? I've begged them for years. Just let me in. Before anyone comes."

She wasn't even listening.

A couple of men ran into the far end of the passage.

Zia said, "Quick, there they are."

She grabbed Tina by the shoulder and pushed her into the access tube to the Freeranger ship.

"Did you hear what I said?" Tina asked.

"You didn't hear what *I* said. You don't want to see them do what I have just witnessed them doing do a group of homeless people. They are not here to talk. The rich boy doesn't care. Artan doesn't care. Shut the door. Take this craft off the station. I've never been more serious about anything in my life."

They really had no option but to take her. Tina slammed the door shut and gave the thumbs up to the young Freeranger man. Finn would be so happy.

But it was not to be helped. The young Freeranger made sure all the safety mechanisms on the door were in the right position. He looked somewhat nervously at the heavily armed guards, but then one of the other crew members started about zero gravity and how they would have to hold on when they left the station.

The normal processes took over. The crew made sure everyone was secured. They strung out the cargo netting so people could hold on.

Apparently, a lot of people were leaving the station, and station control had abandoned their posts, so getting out was not without risk. The pilot engaged the engine in a strong burst, which of course made some people and items fly through the cabin. Apparently one could live on a station without ever having experienced space flight.

It was very crowded in the ship.

They crossed the small section of space to the Freeranger ship. The pilot had turned off the large screen in the cabin. It was stuffy and dark in the cabin.

The pilot spoke to his people on the shipworld and Tina could listen into the conversation, which had a lot of participating voices.

The Freerangers didn't sound terribly happy about the number of newcomers. Several older folk said they'd never agreed to take in this many people, and wanted to make sure that all these people were going to be at the *Manila*, and not and their ship, and that they were going to use the *Manila*'s stores.

Tina didn't know the finer details. They hadn't worked those out yet. Was the *Manila* safe enough? Did Aliz object to having this many civilians on board? She had no idea.

At any rate, they would have a lot of fun eating curry.

The shuttle bypassed the larger Freeranger ship, but pulled right into the *Manila*.

Seated behind the pilot, Tina spotted a structure of lines and cables, presumably for the Freeranger ships to pull the *Manila* along when they left the system.

She would have to check whether Aliz knew where they were going.

The shuttle hovered close to the *Manila*'s docking door, now closed, near the airlock that had malfunctioned and almost killed Tina.

But there were no mishaps this time. The shuttle pilot shot

the line to the hull of the massive ship. One of the Freeranger crew went across.

Yonta had opened the airlock. Tina could see people moving inside, ready to help the passengers across.

It was a very slow process, because each time people crossed, their suits needed to be returned and new people had to get into the suits.

Tina's turn came somewhere halfway in the group. She and Jens went across with three younger passengers.

When they arrived at the *Manila*, the women from the crew were watching, some of them with hope in their eyes. Maybe there were still hoping against hope that Tina would have rescued their mates. But it was Tina's guess that any of those prisoners were well and truly lost.

They got all the refugees on board.

Finn was in the cabin of the *Alethia* and didn't know that his ex was on board yet. She wasn't looking forward to telling him.

It was going to be a long, long journey to safety in a broken ship, with a band of mismatched people, funky supplies, pirates watching from a distance and Dexter threatening to come after her, whatever form that might take.

Aliz sent a message that she wanted Tina at the bridge, so Tina left the transfer of the rest of the passengers to the other crew.

She found Rex at the bridge, where he had been given the task to help plot out a variety of different escape routes.

Apparently, the Freeranger pilots had sent through a couple of potential destinations and travel routes for the fleet. Tina didn't see any location she recognised in the notes. How far were they going to be from Olympus? Would she ever get back to Cayelle?

As the fleet set off on their journey, Tina led the scientists in their first meeting, discussing the different aspects of their upcoming work. They made a plan which included training any non-scientific members of the group to perform work, and building a lab from scratch and gathering all possible information about the infection.

The mountain of work ahead of them was huge, but at least there was now still hope.

When Tina mentioned her meeting with Dexter to Evelle, she said that if he sided with the pirates, she didn't care about him.

Dexter didn't side with the pirates, he led them. He was a big bully on a power trip that had started when she was still married to him.

Tina didn't get the opportunity to speak with Rex until the next morning when they were both at breakfast in the very busy mess, and where Margot spoke about plans to grow their own supplies.

"I saw your dad," Tina said in a low voice. "He was at the station with the pirates."

"I know," Rex said. "He contacted me."

"What did he tell you?"

Rex shrugged. "Not much."

But Tina didn't miss the disturbed look in his eyes. Yes, Dexter had told Rex about procedures to grow him real limbs. Yes, Rex wanted that, badly.

This was going to be a long trip.

Thanks for Reading

THANK you for reading *Project Charon 3: Survival Mode*. As the author of this book, I would hugely appreciate it if you could return to where you purchased it and write a short review. Thanks so much!

The next and final book in this series is Project Charon 4: Swarm

Never again miss a new release and get four books free if you sign up for my newsletter.

ABOUT THE AUTHOR

Patty Jansen lives in Sydney, Australia, where she spends most of her time writing Science Fiction and Fantasy.

Her story *This Peaceful State of War* placed first in the second quarter of the Writers of the Future contest and was published in their 27th anthology. She has also sold fiction to genre magazines such as Analog Science Fiction and Fact, Redstone SF and Aurealis.

Patty has written over thirty novels in both Science Fiction and Fantasy, including the *Icefire Trilogy* and the *Ambassador* series.

pattyjansen.com

BOOKS BY PATTY JANSEN

More information:

PATTYJANSEN.COM

www.ingramcontent.com/pod-product-compliance
Lightning Source LLC
Chambersburg PA
CBHW030804200726
48285CB00014B/656